CHARLY'S
EPICFIASCOS

Reality
Check

Books by Kelli London

Charly's Epic Fiascos series

Charly's Epic Fiascos

Reality Check

Boyfriend Season series

Boyfriend Season

Cali Boys

Stand-Alones

Uptown Dreams

The Break-Up Diaries, Vol. 1 (with Ni-Ni Simone)

Published by Kensington Publishing Corporation

CHARLY'S
EPICFIASCOS

Reality Check

KELLI LONDON

Dafina KTeen Books
KENSINGTON PUBLISHING CORP.
http://www.kensingtonbooks.com

DAFINA KTEEN BOOKS are published by

Kensington Publishing Corp.
119 West 40th Street
New York, NY 10018

ISBN-13: 978-0-7582-8697-0
ISBN-10: 0-7582-8697-X

First Printing: March 2013

10 9 8 7 6 5 4 3 2 1

Printed in the United States of America

Tweet
Chief
Geronimo:

You
three
are
the
center
of
my
universe!

Acknowledgments

To my fantastic trio.

To the world's most loving mom (my mom)!

My family and friends: you know who you are and how much you mean.

Selena James: thanks for everything!

For my readers: As always, I truly and humbly thank you with all of my heart. You're incredible and appreciated.

And for you, *insert your name here*, I thank you for all your support, for reading *all* of my books, and for being the dedicated reader you are. You are truly the best and so amazing.

Take care. Be strong. Love yourself.

Your girl,

Kells
Kellilondon.com

CHARLY

When life gives you lemons, throw them back. It's no law that you have to accept them and make lemonade like the dumb cliché says. Besides, who said that, anyway? Some spineless person who gave in under pressure? Probably. Not me though. I don't follow clichés and I don't accept less. I certainly don't follow rules. Who said that I have to? And who in the heck is Who anyway, that makes everyone follow what Who says? Truth is, I don't know who Who is, and I don't care. I'm Charly with a y, Charly St. James, and that makes me more important than any invisible Who. I make my own rules. I make my own way. I do my thing, and I do it well. At least, I always thought I did, but that day . . . Well, on that day something changed. I knew something was up. Something I wasn't so sure I'd like, but knew I'd deal with because that's my MO (short for modus operandi . . . look it up in the dictionary because it's a snazzy word to know). Anyway, I take trouble, then handle it, because really there's no such thing as a problem. The real definition of a problem is a solution that hasn't been born yet. That's my specialty: making a way out of no way. I just had no idea how I'd be forced to become a master of it, but I was up for it. I had no choice. I'd come too far and wasn't willing to travel backward. But I can say this: traveling by hook or by crook and the 'Hound (i.e., the bus) from just outside of Chicago, Illinois, to Nuevo York (New York) with barely a dollar and a dream was much easier . . . much.

PROLOGUE

There was no way she was staying in. She didn't care what her father said. He hadn't traveled cross-country to capture a dream. She had. And if she got her way today, if she got cast in more than the teensy two-line parts she'd been getting—roles he'd barred her from auditioning for until after she finished online classes for the Internet academy he'd enrolled her in—she'd start in a little over three weeks when school was out for the summer. She tried again to slide open the window in her bedroom. Like her father, the sill was heavy and solid and stubborn, refusing to budge.

"U-ugh!" she growled, backing away from it and swiping her caramel colored hands together as if she were wiping dust off them. "It won't move." She flung her long black hair over her shoulder, then batted her long lashes.

"We told you," her best friend, Lola, sang from the laptop monitor. Her face was too close to the camera, blocking most of Charly's little sister's unblemished face and the restaurant-goers who were blurred in the background. "You're going to have to find another way, Charly."

"Mm-hmm," Stormy agreed, pushing her face against Lola's, vying for camera time. "You can't wiggle open a window that's nailed shut. Try again to remove the nail first, before you break your nails." Stormy laughed.

Lola laughed, then Charly and Stormy joined her. After Charly had moved in with her father, who lived way outside of Manhattan, she'd heard one too many deer or raccoons or whatever it was her father had blamed for the footsteps crunching against the ground. She'd been so scared she'd nailed all the bedroom windows shut. Even after coming to her senses, realizing the animals would stay outside, she was still locked inside because she'd pounded one of the nails too far into the heavy wood frame to remove it. It had become one with the sill.

"Okay. Okay, Charly," Stormy calmed, raising her hand in the air. Her mouth spread into a huge smile. "You see Bathsheba waving behind me?" she asked, then adjusted the monitor so Charly could see.

Charly grinned, waving at Bathsheba, then Smax, her bosses from back home in Illinois. She'd worked for them for quite some time and had become more like family to them than an employee. "Hi, Smax and Bathsheba," she greeted. She could see Smax's long finger waves and gold teeth brighten the screen and Bathsheba pushing him with manicured hands, but she couldn't hear them. By their demeanor, Charly could tell they were fussing with one another.

"They can't hear you," Lola interrupted, "but these people can."

The camera shifted again, and two longtime regular customers appeared on Charly's screen. "Good day, Dr. Deveraux El! Hey, Rudy-Rudy," she greeted the two men. Dr. Deveraux El was a historian who also studied the stars and some other things Charly wasn't so sure of, but he'd been her teacher and friend since the day they'd met, and he seemed to know more about himself than anyone she'd ever met. Rudy-Rudy was a veteran of two wars, who always had a smile and a joke.

"Charly, where ya been all my life?" Rudy-Rudy asked.

"Good evening, Queen Charly," Dr. Deveraux El said. "I'm sending you some study materials. If you haven't learned about the planets in school, I want you to memorize them and know them from the stars. Especially the sun. It's not a planet like everyone thinks, and it doesn't rise and set. The earth does," he said.

Charly just nodded and pasted a huge smile on her face. She was trying to get out of the house, not have a lesson with the good doctor. "Okay." She whispered, "Lola . . . Stormy . . . Come on. I don't have all day. I gotta get out of here."

"Gotcha," Lola said, then turned the monitor back on her and Stormy. "Your dad's gone, right?" she inquired. Charly and her younger sister shared only the same mother, Brigette.

Charly nodded. "Yes. He's out in the shed or something. Somewhere being or playing commando," she said, her expression serious. Her father was supposedly retired military, but Charly knew better. Her dad hadn't really retired, or the government didn't know the meaning of the word, because they wouldn't fully let him go. They were always calling him for something—something that told Charly he was not to be tricked or toyed with, because he refused to talk about whatever he specialized in.

Lola fingered her naturally blond porcupine hairdo and rolled her authentic ocean-blue eyes. "Did you hear what you just said, Charly?"

Charly snapped her fingers. She'd been so paranoid about her father finding out that she had planned to audition without his knowledge or permission, she hadn't given enough thought to sneaking out. "So why not just walk out the front door?" she said, asking the question aloud instead of in her head, which would've been cooler. She nodded. "He just knows there'll be an audition *some*day. He doesn't know on what day," she explained to everyone, smiling at the face that'd popped up next to Lola's on her computer monitor. "And it's not a real audition, is it? So it doesn't count."

"Go 'head, baby. You can do it," said the only voice she needed to make her move. *Mason.* Her boo. He was ultra fine and sweet, and had roped her in with his swag, then they'd hooked up—well, almost hooked up, right before she'd headed East to pursue her acting career, but distance didn't keep him out of her dreams. "Remember what you told me, Charly. You didn't go all the way to New York for nothing. You said your dream wouldn't wait."

"And it won't," she assured herself more than anyone else, then picked up Marlow, her caramel and white Shih Tzu, from the floor. "I'm taking Marlow for a walk.

That's what I'll tell my dad if I run into him. I'll hit you guys up by cell—especially you, Mason," she said, then closed the video chat, powered off her computer, and headed out to audition for her dream role. It may not have been the reality television show she'd moved to New York to get, the one that had been cancelled after they'd shot the pilot, but it would have to do. Television was television, and no matter how it was spelled, the opportunity to be on it spelled D-R-E-A-M to Charly.

Her nerves were a mess. A pure, blown-out-of-proportion, rattling battle of right versus wrong had ping-ponged in her head since she'd snuck through the back-door of the studio. She knew better than to sneak on the sitcom set and pretend to be one of the actors, but she couldn't help it. She'd come for a reason, and backing out of her fake-it-and-hopefully-you'll-make-it plan wasn't it. So when the production assistant called for the cast to ready themselves, she moved with the group. Now Charly sat facing the front of the set, on the bright orange, hard plastic bus seat with her legs crossed and Marlow on her lap. She looked forward where the staged bus driver's seat was located, then averted her eyes to her lap and thumbed through a magazine as if she'd belonged there. She popped the gum in her mouth. A couple of transit riders moved to and fro and up and down the makeshift bus aisle, grabbing an available seat and swaying from side to side as if they were trying to prevent themselves from falling. One person stood, grabbing the long cord, then pulled it until it made a dinging noise, signaling they wanted off. Charly, while pretending to read the magazine, managed to glance at the no-names. They were dressed awful and their acting was worse.

The "bus" stopped and the passengers got off.

"No more local stops after this," the driver yelled. "The last stop is the end of the line."

Charly huffed, folding the magazine and getting a grip on Marlow. "Midge," she called to the driver, "I know you said no more local stops, but I need to get off at the next corner. You hear me, Midge?" she asked, waiting to be recognized.

The driver turned and stared directly in Charly's face, giving her no acknowledgment.

Charly grabbed Marlow and the folded magazine, jumped up from her seat, then made her way to the front where Midge sat. "Midge, didn't you hear me? I said I gotta get off. I gotta save Bobby," Charly urged.

Midge let go of the wheel and turned her whole body to face Charly. She got up and put her hands on her hips. "Who in the world is *Bobby*? Who are *you*?" she asked.

"Cut. Cut!" a producer yelled. "Somebody tell me who this actor is," he said, flipping through the script he held. "What did I miss? The driver has a name now? And what about the dog? There's a dog? I don't see that scene written in anywhere. And I certainly don't see a Bobby either! Who's she again? And what is she uh . . . doing? Her acting is . . . ugh." He turned his hand side to side as if saying *so-so*. "What is it, method?" he asked Charly.

"Improv," Charly yelled, then gulped when she saw who walked onto the set from a door in the back. She locked eyes with an outraged Mr. Day, the man who'd discovered her after she'd snuck into the audition he'd held months ago that had prompted her to move to the city, then shrugged her shoulders. She twisted her expression into a look that said she was sorry, then averted her eyes. The big studio seemed smaller now. The open ceilings with exposed metal beams and expanse of space with cameras and lights and people surrounding it in a horseshoe fashion now seemed claustrophobic. The vastness and crowdedness that had made it easy for her to sneak in and blend with the real actors was now turning on her, and so was everyone's attention. Charly inhaled.

"Charly! Charly?" Mr. Day yelled, walking toward the set and adjusting his fitted baseball hat over his electric grayish-white hair. He shook his head in disbelief. "I step out for just a few minutes, then walk back in and see you here. Do you realize that you just tried to audition for a sitcom? That's impossible. This is a sitcom—a casted sitcom—not an audition—but you know that, don't you?"

Charly nodded, then began petting Marlow. "Life is an audition, Mr. Day."

His eyes pierced hers, making her quiet. "How many times do I have to tell you that I have another project in the works? One I think may be good for you, if it pans out?"

Charly walked off the set and over to him. "But I can't wait for *if*, Mr. Day. You know that. The other show you'd planned was good on paper, but the pilot was even better than I'd imagined—so was the commercial. I don't know why the studio cancelled it. I didn't come to New York—"

"For nothing . . . I know. How can I forget your words: *for nothing*?" Mr. Day finished for her, rubbing his hand along his jawline. "And *cancel* isn't the right word for the last show—the attempted show. They didn't pick it up, Charly. They didn't pick it up because it wasn't time." He paused. "One second, Charly," he said, turning to a production assistant who'd called out to him.

Just as Mr. Day turned away from her, Charly noticed a hush come over the set before loud whispers started. That could only mean one thing—a star was on the scene. But who? That's when she spotted the entourage of well-dressed helpers, and in their midst was Miss A herself.

"No way . . ." she said, zeroing in on one of the biggest actresses to ever hit the small screen. Annison. She'd been a rising star for Disney, then all of the sudden she'd disappeared after her sister had hit the big-time in a big way thanks to their hot shot television network dad, who had a way of making sure his kids reached their dreams. Even Annison's brother, who barely had talent, had snatched the limelight. Charly sighed. If only her father headed up a movie studio the way Annison's father did—she'd have people whispering and cameras flashing her photo too. As Charly took in the star's outfit, she wondered where the girl shopped. Her clothes didn't look like they'd come off a rack. She thought about asking her, but she couldn't just run over and talk Annison, could she? No. That would be too cheesy, too stalker-like. Just as Charly started to turn away, Annison waved in her direction. Or at least she thought it was her direction. Charly nodded her head in return, not wanting to look silly by returning a wave meant for someone else.

Mr. Day turned back to her. "Okay, Charly. It's time

for you to go home. Do you have a ride or do you need to call your dad?"

She cradled Marlow. "I have a ride," she lied.

Mr. Day rubbed his hand across the top of her head, purposely messing up her hair. He nodded, then shook his head. "No, Charly, you don't have a ride. And we both know it. You don't have to lie to me. When are you finally going to get it through this thick skull of yours that I'm on your side?"

"When you give me a role," Charly admitted.

"I can't give you a role just yet, but you can stay on the set. You know, see what it's like—"

Charly cut him off. "So let me earn a role. I'm at the set now." She wasn't trying to be smart, she just felt he needed reminding.

Mr. Day grimaced, then rolled his eyes in a masculine, you're-getting-on-my-nerves way. "That's it. I'm calling your father. You need a ride home. Didn't he say no acting until school's out, anyway? Summer break is right around the corner, Charly. Have some patience." He walked away, whipping out his BlackBerry.

Charly turned on her heels, strutting away with her head held high. "Patience doesn't cut it. Persistence does," she mumbled.

GETTING TO FAMOUS

1

Attitudes were flaring, and the pressure was on. Time was ticking, and every minute cost thousands of dollars. "Move it! Move it! We're behind schedule, people!" a production assistant boomed, her hand waving to and fro. Costumers shuttled rolling wardrobes across the floor. Cameramen yelled, some cursing. Extras huddled together, inching forward toward the set, though they'd been told not to. Charly stood to the side, watching and holding Marlow. It was a mess. A certifiable yet beautiful disaster was unfolding in front of her, but she didn't care. Mr. Day hadn't told on her weeks ago like he'd threatened to. He hadn't said one word to her father. Instead, today he'd sent a car to retrieve her and Marlow so she could familiarize herself with the set and production crew, and so Marlow could get used to all the busyness. He had promised her "big things," so she knew it was only a matter of time before the disorder was fine-tuned

into something fit for television. Now she was just waiting for it all to develop, so she could see what Mr. Day
had in store for her with some new upcoming reality series he'd been so hush-hush about and, more importantly,
so she could hurry afterward to the airport to meet
Mason's plane, which was due in just after two o'clock.
She smiled, calming and reminding herself why she was
here and how much she'd gone through to make it. She'd
traveled from the Midwest to New York, pit-stopping in
what she'd come to refer to as levels of purgatory, to capture an opportunity such as this, and now that it had pre-
sented itself, she was going to own it. No matter what.

"What are you standing there for, man? We got work
to do," a guy with a producer badge around his neck asked
flippantly, clipboard in his hands. "Let's go!" Charly
strained to see the object of the producer's wrath, feeling
sorry for whomever he was talking to. She was glad he
wasn't snapping at her, because for the life of her, she didn't
know how she'd have responded to such a bullying tone.
But she knew it wouldn't have been nice.

"*Did* you hear me, man? I. Said. We. Have. Work. To.
Do. Now, c'mon!" he urged, waving the clipboard. "Okay.
It's not gonna be my butt on the line . . ." He trailed off
with an unspoken threat.

Charly looked left and right, hoping that whoever
would hurry up. The producer's impatience was making
her uncomfortable.

"He seems upset, doesn't he?" a male voice asked from
behind, startling her and tickling her eardrums with an
English accent.

Charly glanced over her shoulder and nodded to the

guy's shadow behind her. Too entertained by the producer to divert her attention all the way, she didn't see his
face. "Yeah. But I think that's an understatement," she
agreed, quickly turning her glance back to the angry producer, who was reddening by the second. She was sure
that in less than a minute the man was going to drag
whoever he was yelling at across the floor to wherever he
wanted him.

"Hey, Day! Day! Mr. Day?" the producer guy yelled,
almost throwing his clipboard in the air. "I thought you
said we have a live one. Where is he?"

An irritating, mic-held-too-close-to-the-speakers sound
fractured the air, making everyone wince and cover their
ears. Suddenly it stopped, then was replaced by a crack-
ling noise, followed by "Testing? One. Two. Testing?" blar-
ing through a bullhorn.

"Charly? Charly?" Mr. Day's voice called from somewhere behind the cameras.

Charly perked up and stood on tiptoe, trying to see
past the cameras and crew. She pointed to her chest like
she'd forgotten her name. "Me?" she mouthed out of
habit. Having what was considered a common male
name, she'd learned long ago not to assume someone was
talking to her.

"Yes, you, Charly," Mr. Day assured her. "I'm talking
to you, and so is Ryan. The man in front of you with the
clipboard. He's the producer."

Now her eyes really widened, then locked with the
producer's. "Me?" she mouthed again, clutching Marlow
in one arm and pointing to her chest again. She didn't
understand. Why were they calling her? This time she'd

come to watch, not participate. The last time she partici-
pated, Mr. Day had run her out and had threatened to
tell her dad, and with good reason. She'd popped up and
auditioned during a real taping.

The scrumptious male voice behind her laughed.
"Oops. Guess you are the *man* who's pissed off Ryan. I
wouldn't want to be in your shoes," he said, his *off*
sounding like *awff*.

Ryan's eyes saucered wider than Charly's. "You?" he
asked incredulously. "All this time I was looking for a he,
not a her. And definitely not an *it*," he said, pointing at
Marlow. "Well, same difference. Let's go!" he yelled,
walking toward Charly and extending his arm. "Time is
money, and we don't have either to waste. Hair and
makeup. Wardrobe!" he called out, gently taking Charly
by the hand.

She looked at his reddened face, and thought his gentle
hold on her was so contradictory. "I don't understand,"
she said, clasping her hand with Ryan's like she was lost.
"Mr. Day sent for me so I can watch. You know, learn?
I've been banned . . ." She glanced over her shoulder to
where the delicious voice had come from, and her eyes
took over. The guy with the accent was gorgeous. Hand-
some, beautiful, cute, and whatever other words could be
used to describe a guy who was so fine, he was all of
that. She blinked slowly, trying to pull her attention
from him, but she couldn't. He was magnetic, attractive,
model-tall, and had the perfect build. He was cut like a
triathlete, and his muscular build was topped off with delectable biceps. ". . . and can only watch . . . there's no
getting in front of the camera for a while. I can only

watch . . . only watch," she stuttered, repeating her words. She didn't know what to say or do, not after looking at the guy.

"Uh-huh. Tell that to hair and makeup and wardrobe—aka the Gossip Trinity. They love to hear stories . . . and spread them too. I, on the other hand, love to *see* stories. Action. I'm here to make it all happen." His voice was incredibly loud, as if she were across the room and not next to him. He looked at her and smirked. "I don't do excuses, babe. And I don't do dogs. I do production." He stood straight, looking around as if he hadn't been speaking to her. "Someone get this dog. Now!"

"Wait a second. Don't talk to me like that! And definitely don't call Marlow an *it*! She's a her. Do you hear me?" she began, but before Charly could finish instructing the producer, Ryan, on what he could kiss and how he could kiss it, he looked her up and down, taking her all in. "Suede boots and striped tights while it's warm—trendsetter, huh? Gutsy and edgy." He winked and nodded, in what seemed like approval. "Cute, confident, conflict-worthy, and cutting edge. Charly," he said at the top of his lungs, then handed her off to a group of stylists who she assumed were the Gossip Trinity. "Who knows, Day?" Ryan yelled to Mr. Day. "You may be on to something here with this *Ms.* Charly St. James. She's quite the character and very expressive too. She wears her feelings on her face—looked at me like *You know where you can go!* And trust me, the look wasn't directing me to heaven! Ha! Cameras may love her." He shrugged. "Then again, they may not," he said as if Charly weren't right there to hear him.

"What are you talking about?" she asked snidely. "Mr. Day!" she yelled. "Somebody better tell me what's up or I'm walking or swinging fists. The first person that touches me I'm touching back."

Mr. Day was in her face before she knew it. "Calm down, Charly. It was supposed to be a surprise, but I guess I might as well tell you. We're doing the show. *You*'re doing the show," he said.

Her index finger was pointed to her chest again. "Me? What show?"

Mr. Day laughed. "Now you get it. Just get ready. I'll meet you in the dressing room to explain. But think *Extreme Makeover: Home Edition* meets something even more fantastic."

Fingers were in her long hair. A makeup color palette was held up to her face, and measuring tape encircled her waist while small hands tried to free Marlow from Charly's grasp. "Wait," Charly protested, stomping her foot, locking her limbs, and tightening her hold on Marlow. Everything and everyone was moving too fast, and she still didn't completely understand what was going on. She knew she was going to do a series, but was taken aback at the rush of it all. "*Who* are you and *what* are you trying to do with Marlow?" she asked a small woman who had her tiny hands around Marlow's body.

The lady smiled. "I'm the vet, Ms. St. James. We're just going to give her a quick checkup. Make sure she has all her shots so she can be on the set, then it's off for a shampoo and groom."

"Diva St. James, your dog's in better hands than anyone on the set, trust me," the guy with the tape measure around her waist assured her, looking up into her eyes. "Doc Peta here will take good care of him—"

"Her. Marlow's a *her*," Charly corrected, cutting him off.

"Well, Diva St. James, Doc Peta here—and yes, Peta is her name and, of course, her affiliation too."

"But that'd be in all caps, Ramone. The affiliation is in all caps. People for the Ethical Treatment of Animals would be capitalized," the girl with the color palette corrected. "Would that be considered a homonym then?" she asked no one. "You're a number thirty-five foundation, Ms. St. James."

"Anyway," Ramone said, shrugging off color-palette-girl's comment. "Like I was saying, Diva St. James, Marlow's in good hands."

Charly looked at the village who'd been sent to take care of her and Marlow. "Charly. Not Ms. St. James. Not Diva St. James. Everyone, call me Charly, please."

Ramone's eyebrows shot to the heavens, and the rest of the village gasped. "Oh . . . kay. Charly? *Really?* Just Charly?" he asked, nodding, then smiled. The others followed suit, and Doc Peta pinched Charly's cheek like she was a baby.

Charly didn't know what the big deal was. Charly was her name, after all. "Yes. Really. Charly."

"My pleasure," he said, then stood and laced his arm through hers. "Well, *Charly*, now that you know Marlow's in good hands, come so we can work you over with our even better hands. With this thin waist, pretty face, and goo-gobs of hair you have, we'll make the cameras love you more than anyone else. Everyone else. Especially your costars, the guy and the girl. The guy you should watch out for. He's mean, and the girl . . . well, she thinks she's a diva. But you'll be better. That's our mission. Trust me." He led her toward the back of the studio and outside, where the makeup and dressing trailers were. Charly wanted to ask him who and what he was talking about, but he just kept on talking and talking, and didn't give her time to inquire.

The Gossip Trinity had stuck Charly's head in a bowl, shampooed, then rolled and unrolled most of her hair, only to finger-roll the loose tendrils into pinwheel curls, which they coiled and pinned to her head with a mere, "We'll let it set, then style it after you're dressed." Ramone, the obvious leader of the trio, was the dresser and head stylist and he wrapped her in outfit after outfit until he found what he'd called "one worthy of wearing Charly," then instructed, "From here on out, you don't wear clothes. Your clothes wear you. Clothes are merely accessories, my dear. *You* are the wardrobe that the accessories complement." He looked around, ignoring Charly as if he hadn't just spoken to her. "Someone please put more rollers in her hair. And add some pieces too. Her natural hair's too heavy to hold curls, and it's too long for pins."

Charly now sat in a chair in front of the mirror, with her back turned on her reflection while someone wove in pieces of fake hair with her already long hair, then added more rollers. She was surrounded by the Gossip Trinity and other onlookers. Her face was turned left, then right while some people nodded yes and others no. Not seeing herself was killing her. Not knowing what was going on was making her want to kill someone. Losing control of herself and life and choices for the last two hours wasn't normal for her, but then again, her life had never known normal, especially since she'd ventured to capture her dream months ago.

Three slow, deliberate handclaps pulled her attention from her audience, shifting her focus to the door. Mr. Day walked toward her, nodding and smiling. "You are something else, Charly. Like Ryan said, the cameras are going to love you."

"Thank you," Ramone said, proudly taking credit. "We told her."

Mr. Day gave a dismissive nod to Ramone.

"Whatever . . . Charly will be the hottest thing in front of the camera. Period," Ramone mumbled, loud enough for Charly to hear but low enough to escape Mr. Day's ears.

Charly's eyebrows drew together while she waited for the girl to finish rolling her hair. With all hands finally off her, she pushed her palms against the chair's armrests to stand up. "Mr. Day. Listen. Enough is enough is enough, already. You told me you'd fill me in. Now, fill me in. What's this show about?" she asked, exasperated. "And where is Marlow?"

Mr. Day smiled, then snapped his fingers. "What's wrong, Charly? Afraid of getting what you want?" he whispered, then smiled, turning away. "I'm ready for her. Please get her and send her in," he said to someone Charly couldn't see, who was standing in the trailer's three-step stairwell. He pointed to the style trio and their assistants. "Give us five."

"Get who? Tell me why I'm here again?" She felt as if she were parroting herself, but she had to know.

Charly watched as the small group, whom she referred to as her village, hustled out of the trailer with an "Oh! Excuse us," then mumbled, "This is going to be interesting. Clash of the divas."

Mr. Day adjusted his baseball cap over his electric grayish-white hair, then crossed his arms over his chest. A huge smile spread his lips. "Well, getting familiar with the set was the plan. But plans change . . . and, fortunately for you, so do *reality* shows. This one is way better, and the studio is behind it. Big-time. In fact, there will be no pilot. This is the real deal and there are already sponsors. We're talking commercials, products, you name it, we got it. They're even beginning to market it." He nodded. "Yep. And we've also got big names attached to it too. A big one-named star who's getting ready to shine again. Some people just can't be held back."

Charly tilted her head, trying to grasp what he was saying. The show she'd been slated for had been cancelled, which had been a huge disappointment. They'd shot a pilot, even a commercial, but then, nothing. The network had changed their mind, and Charly was left waiting. And Mr. Day had kept hinting about another show, but never revealed anything. "Okay . . . ?" she began, then her jaw hit the floor as his words sunk in. *Really?*

"Yep," Mr. Day said as if reading her mind. "And since your contract has that option clause, your mother pretty much sealed the deal. By law—though it's not as simple as I'm going to make this sound—you owe the studio a show," he began, then filled Charly in on the show while they waited.

Charly was so excited. The show was going to be huge. She knew it because she felt it. "So I get to help teenagers? That's cool. But what do they have to do to qualify?"

Mr. Day looked her dead in the eyes. "Think of a great Samaritan—not a good one, but a great one. Think of someone who helps everyone else, is deserving of a good life but hasn't had a break. Well, that's what you'll be, Charly. You'll be the break they've been waiting for."

The beautiful girl Charly had grown up watching on television and on the big screen entered the trailer, interrupting Mr. Day, then walked over and stood in front of her. She wore jeans with stylish rips in them, courtesy of a high-end designer, a plain white baby tee with spaghetti straps and a long, red summer scarf that danced in the air. On her head was a pair of oversized sunglasses. Her hair was pulled back in a sloppy ponytail, and her face was minus makeup or expression. Seconds seemed like minutes as the girl stared at Charly, tapping a flip-flopped foot on the floor. She said not one word. Finally, she nodded.

"Annison," Charly whispered.

Mr. Day beamed, snaking his neck so he could see around Charly, who'd walked in front of him and was now blocking his view. "Yes? Is that a yes?"

Annison removed her sunglasses, then took Charly in, pressing her lips together in thought. She nodded. "She'll do." Then she smiled, big and wide and forcefully, like she'd been practicing it. Her eyes were void of feeling." Yes, that's a yes."

Charly looked from the starlet to Mr. Day, then back to the girl. She wasn't just your normal, everyday girl. She was Annison. Annison had been like the Nikkis and Waynes of the world, then suddenly she seemed to disappear. Obviously she was back, and was just as beautiful and commanding of attention as ever. "Yes? Yes, what?" Charly asked Annison, turning to Mr. Day, then back to Annison.

Annison proffered her hand. Her smile was still intact, her teeth were bright, and her attitude matched. She seemed warm in a strictly-for-the-camera way. "Nice to meet you, Charly. I'm Annison—"

"Oh. I know. Trust me, I know who you are. *Every*one does," Charly said, almost jumping out of her boots. She couldn't contain her excitement. She'd never been so close to such a big star, and was floored that Annison knew her and called her by her name.

Mr. Day stood like a proud father, looking from one girl to the other. He nodded. "You were right, Annison. Charly's a great match for you."

Charly, still holding Annison's hand, froze. "Match?"

Annison shrugged and pressed her lips together. "Yes. I have good taste. I knew you'd be, well . . . good. I saw the pilot of the show you were in that was canceled, which is too bad. You were good. Then when you crashed that sitcom and were on the bus and kept calling the driver Midge, I knew you were the one."

Charly nodded. "Thank you." So she'd been right. That had been Annison she saw on the set.

Mr. Day smiled. "Charly, meet the star—"

Annison loudly cleared her throat.

"Sorry. I meant to say, Charly, Annison's the star of a new show: *The Extreme Dream Team*, a traveling reality series where some lucky person's life is made over. And you're going to be on it with Annison!"

Annison cleared her throat again.

"Sorry. You're going to be Annison's costar!" he announced.

Charly couldn't breathe. Costar? She'd take co-whatever. As long as she was co-something, she was happy. Before she knew it, she'd clasped her arms around the actress. She was glad that Annison had chosen her to do the show, which meant the director of the sitcom had been wrong. Here he'd questioned Charly's method of acting when she'd pretended to be a cast member, even implied it wasn't so good, but he'd been everything but right. If she'd acted badly, Annison wouldn't have chosen her, she told herself.

Annison pulled away and put both her hands on Charly's shoulders. She smiled. "You're welcome," she said, then put her sunglasses back on with one hand and reached into an oversized bag on her shoulder. She pulled out a small box and handed it to Charly. "It's nothing, just a little welcome and thank-you." She turned to Mr. Day. "Day. I'm ready. Where's my crew and my trailer? You did get the crew I requested, right?" she asked, walking toward the door and glancing at her watch. "There's no need for me to be fitted and styled. My crew already knows what I need, and besides, I've been acting for*ever* so I don't do camera warm-ups, and reality TV doesn't

call for run-throughs—there are no lines to rehearse."
She paused, then turned to face Mr. Day and Charly, a
look of worry on her face. "I have a two-o'clock yoga
class, and it's almost one thirty." She glanced at Charly,
who was turning over the slim box in her hands. "Are
you a yogi, Charly?"

Charly nodded, then shook her head. No, she wasn't.
In fact, nothing about yoga had ever excited her, and she
couldn't understand why people rushed to a place to
stretch when they could stretch at home for free. It couldn't
be that hard, and if that's what it took to better the show, if
that's what Annison did to stay in such great shape, she
could learn. "Not yet, but I've always been interested. I
heard it works wonders," Charly lied, finally opening the
box. Inside was a shock of red. Charly reached in and removed a long silk scarf. "This is beautiful. A summer
scarf, like yours?"

Annison gave a half nod. "Yes, to the scarf and yoga.
Scarves and oversized sunglasses are for starlets, and
yoga does a body good," she said, looking over her own
ballerina-type physique. She shrugged. "Well, you have
the scarf now. Sunglasses are easy to get. Maybe one day
I can invite you out to the yoga shala. We do yoga daily,
but it's kinda a private, sisters-only group. We'll see.
Gotta go," she said, then turned and walked down the
stairs and disappeared. Mr. Day scampered behind her.

Charly stood in awe with her mouth hanging open and
her heart palpitating. She was caught somewhere between excitement about getting to work with such a big
star and almost being invited to work out with her. Charly's
eyes bulged. She looked at her watch and her heart danced.

Mason would be arriving in New York shortly, and she had to be at the airport to meet him when his plane touched down. She'd promised him, and she didn't go back on her word. She hoped he didn't go back on his either. He'd promised to bring her some of her favorite chocolate-popcorn from a mom-and-pop joint in Chicago, and her mouth had been watering for it all morning. "I'm sorry, but I gotta go too!" she yelled toward Mr. Day's back, and began taking off her robe.

Ramone and the rest of the Gossip Trinity who were assigned to her beauty needs hustled back into the trailer. "Where are you going?" Ramone asked.

"I gotta get to the airport. Fast. And I need to leave Marlow here." She looked at him, then to the next person, then to the next. "Anyone have a car?"

Ramone shook his head. "This is New York. No one has a car. We have trains and taxis and bikes and personal drivers, so why would we have cars? Cars, for the most part, are a waste of money and space in New York. Besides, have you seen how much parking is here?"

"Ramone, get off it. It's time to trade in your diaper. That's not true for everyone. Some of us do have cars, and they're not always a waste of money. Not for me," a very deep voice said from behind, making everyone turn around. The first thing Charly noticed was tattoos.

The Gossip Trinity greeted him, apparently knowing who the guy was, and egged Charly on that it was cool to ride with him.

Ramone sucked his teeth. "This is who I was talking about, Charly. He's mean, but I guess he's all right once you get to know him." He turned his attention back to the guy. "And get off what? And trade in my *what*? What did you say? You're always a handful."

"Get off your pedestal, man—the one you've been on since whoever you dress sends their personal driver to pick you up," the tattooed guy pointed out without a care. "And I'm referring to your diaper, Ramone. Trade it in, get you some big-boy boxers, and stop being such a baby. You're always whining and being cynical. Just because you break yourself on designer clothes and after parties, doesn't mean everyone else can't afford a car."

Ramone made the sound with his teeth again, then waved away the comment. His voice was silent, but his attitude was loud. "Ridiculous. Good thing you're an actor; maybe you can act like you have a good attitude sometimes," he mumbled.

Charly looked at the guy, trying to figure out who he was. He seemed familiar, but she couldn't pinpoint why. He was super skinny, with very expressive eyes, and the skin on his face had a dull tone. The rest of his body seemed to be covered in tattoos, at least the uncovered parts that she could see. She guessed he had to be under five nine, five eight if he was lucky, and something about him, even from a distance, told her she'd like him. Maybe it was his directness or the grimacelike smile he flashed at her, then at everyone else. It seemed everyone in the trailer knew him, but no one was calling him by his name. All she knew was that by what she could hear of his deep voice, he definitely wasn't the dude with the English accent, but he was friendly and warm in a kind-of-like-a-cousin way, but he was no boy-next-door. He was naturally rude and grungy looking and had huge holes in his ears that were fitted with specialized earrings. He wore a tattered fisherman hat that had seen better days. Charly nodded. Yes, he was different, but his grin was wide and genuine and welcoming. But, she told herself, there was no way she could get in a car with him. He was a stranger, and even if she didn't find him attractive, she had a boyfriend, a boyfriend who probably wouldn't like her riding to the airport with a guy she didn't know. She shook her head. There was no way she could let this guy take her to meet Mason.

"I'm Sully, one of the cohosts slash costars slash co-whatever-they-want-to-call-us-so-we'll-feel-special of the show," he said, introducing himself and mockingly rolling his eyes while approaching her. "Come on. I'll take you. Since we're going to be traveling together for the show, we might as well get to know each other. Right?" He tapped the tattooed watch on his left arm. "And besides, you seem to be in a rush. Do you know what time it is?" He held out his other arm to her, where he wore a real watch.

Charly grabbed his right wrist, pulling it toward her, hoping she wouldn't break him. He was that slender. She grunted. Time wasn't her friend at the moment, and she had to get to Mason. "Okay, Sully. Let's go."

2

The ride to the airport had been short and eventful, she thought, finally breathing easier. Sully, to her surprise, was major cool in his own rude, sarcastic way, and had kept her laughing the whole time. She knew for a fact that whoever had cast Sully for the series was good at selecting people. The cameras would love him with his tattooed skin and expressive eyes—and so would the audience, she thought with a laugh.

"What? What did I miss?" he asked, turning his monster truck with huge, oversized tires onto the long strip that led to the airport.

"It's nothing . . ." she lied.

"Liar!" he called out, then laughed when she reddened.

Charly laughed, holding up her hand. "Please stop it, Sully. Please? You've had me in stitches the whole ride."

Sully nodded, speeding up behind a long line of vehicles headed toward the sign that read BAGGAGE CLAIM. He threw her a forced mean look. "If you don't share . . ." His words trailed off in an unspoken threat.

"I was just thinking that whoever cast you for the show knew what they were doing. You're hilarious, and the audience is going to eat you up—that's how much they're going to love you." Charly grinned.

"Ah . . . already becoming a producer," Sully said, nodding. His tone was semi-sarcastic and knowing. "That's cool, Charly. Don't get locked in on one side of the cameras, because there's more on the other side," he said. "That's what my dad always told me because I've wanted to be a star forever. And my dad should know; he's into media marketing. You know, like commercials on steroids—NFL Super Bowl type of marketing—but all the time. Think Times Square and prime time all over the globe."

They pulled alongside the curb, inching their way behind a traffic jam. Charly looked at the clock on the dash and saw she had some time. "Really? That's cool." She grinned.

He shrugged. "If you say so. It's all right, I guess. If you like twenty-three hours a day, six days a week, instead of twenty-four-seven, meaning my pops is only available for the fam one hour a day and one day a week, not twenty-four-seven like he should be. But somebody's gotta pay the bills, right?" He threw her a look that said *don't comment.*

"Well, that's more than I can say about my—never mind," Charly said, deciding not to share too much. She didn't know Sully well enough to tell him about her still absent mom and once absent dad or let him get in her business.

He nodded. "Well, if you really think it's cool, you'll see how cool soon," Sully said matter-of-factly. Traffic finally started to move, and he threw her a quick wink, then pulled the monster truck behind a line of taxis inching their way closer to the airport terminal.

Charly grabbed her purse from the backseat, thinking about their entire conversation and how it'd made her feel. It was nice to know someone who'd wanted something as badly as she and said whatever was on their mind just as she did, and even better to know he'd be on the road with the show. With his rude words and tattooed skin, she was certain he would distract attention away from her blatant honesty that others often misconstrued as crassness.

"You sure you don't want me to wait for you?" he asked, adjusting his fisherman hat and pulling up to one of the entrances.

Charly shook her head and pulled the handle to open the door. "Thanks, Sully, but I'm okay. I really appreciate the ride," she said, climbing down from the truck. There was no way she was going to let Mason see her with him. Not after Sully had made her laugh so hard. She didn't want Mason to misconstrue her having a good time with a fellow actor to mean more than it was. Plus, Sully was too frail looking, and she didn't want Mason to take advantage of Sully's size and test him. She shook her head. Why was she even thinking this way? Mason was secure and had never shown her an ounce of jealousy before. It had to be the distance making her feel guilty and question his feelings.

"Tomorrow, then?" Sully asked while she was shutting the door.

She paused mid-swing. "Tomorrow?"

He nodded. "Yes. Tomorrow. How are you on the show and don't know what's going on? Never mind."

Charly shook her head. "Sully, before we part, let me tell you who I am." She pursed her lips together. "In case you haven't noticed yet, I'm not like Ramone or anyone else on the show, I'm betting. Think of me as the female you. I don't play, either. So please don't mock me—don't speak to me like that." She nodded. " 'Kay. We got an understanding?" Her hand was on one hip.

Sully nodded, then smiled. " 'Bout time I met my match." He winked again. "Anyway, female me, we have to do a run-through with a mock set; that way we kind of get a feel for next week. You do know we're hitting the road next week?" He held up his hands. "And I'm not being smart. Well, I'm always smart, I'm just not being a smart A."

Charly nodded, appreciating his getting the point and not testing her. She didn't really feel like snapping on him or anyone at the moment. She was picking up the love of her life, and her mood was good.

"Oh, Charly?" he said. "One more thing, just in case you didn't know. You didn't really need my watch to tell you you're running late. You have on your own."

Charly laughed. She looked at her wrist, then shook her

head. She'd forgotten she had on a watch. And she had no idea the show was hitting the road so soon, and neither did Mason, who she hoped wouldn't be disappointed, because she'd promised that they would hang out for a couple of weeks without interruption. But then again, she told herself, he'd be happy for her. How could he not? He'd be just as thrilled for her as she was about getting the chocolate, caramel, and pecan–covered popcorn he was bringing her. Besides, he was her biggest supporter. "Tomorrow," she assured Sully, smiling and shutting the truck door, then rushed into the terminal.

She was going to kiss him. Definitely. There was no way around it, and she didn't care who saw. She'd changed in a real way, and was now the person he'd always thought her to be. Strong. Confident. The girl who had it all together. Yes, she was all those things now, thanks to New York and the time they'd had to build their relationship over the phone and through text messages. Charly shook her head and laughed, surprised at how much she'd grown. The scene had changed. Majorly. She was no longer afraid of anything, especially Mason. He'd once made her nervous and too timid to be her real self, but that was in the past. It was what it was now, and she was going to take full advantage of all she could make it be between them. And at the top of her to-do-with-Mason list was a long hug, then an almost-grown kiss.

Charly paced the floor, dragging the long red silky scarf behind her as she made it to one end of the baggage claim area, then about-faced and walked to the other. Time was killing her, ticking by slowly. She'd been anticipating this day for a long time, and it just wasn't happening fast enough. Where was he? she wondered, looking toward the entrance. Mason should've arrived by now. She looked at the watch she'd forgotten she'd worn, urging it to speed up. But no matter how hard she tried, she couldn't force the second hand to move any faster.

"Excuse me? Miss?" a small voice cut through the noisy area.

Charly kept pacing, looking for Mason to appear out of the crowd that'd just entered the baggage claim area. Rising up on tiptoe, she looked for a delicious shade of chocolate topped by a navy baseball hat with NY embroidered on it, the hat she'd bought and sent him.

"Excuse me?" the small voice said again.

Something was tugging on Charly's shirt, and she turned. A young girl, no more than twelve or thirteen, was pulling on her. Charly's brows rose and her expression turned blank. Who was this kid and why was she grabbing her? Charly cleared her throat. "Yes? Do I know you?"

"Charly?"

Charly tilted her head. How did this little girl know her name? "Yes?"

"I knew it was you. I remember you from TV. You were just on like a couple of hours ago."

Charly's heart caught in her throat. *Television?* The girl had to be mistaken because she hadn't been on television in a while, not since her last walk-on—that's how she liked to refer to her two- and three-line parts. But how else could the girl know her name? she wondered. "Really? When? You sure?" she asked, remembering Mr. Day had said the studio had already begun marketing the show. She hadn't expected it to move so fast.

Suddenly, a group of girls walked up. Cute teenagers who obviously were friends of the first girl because they all squealed together, then laughed and smiled. "Oh, it is you. We had a bet," one of them said.

Charly just smiled and nodded. She'd never before received the star treatment, and didn't know how to deal with it. "You did?" she began, then trailed off, spotting Mason. She waved her arm in the air until she got his attention, then beckoned him over, not wanting to be rude and walk away from the group of girls.

"Yes," they sang.

Mason walked up, his eyes large and his grin equal to everyone else's but smoother. "Hey, baby," he said, then pecked Charly on her cheek. His stare zoomed in on her, then he shook his head, laughing. He adjusted his baseball hat and straightened his computer bag on his shoulder. He looked at the group of girls. "What's up?"

"Hi," the girls greeted before Charly could. "Are you Charly's boyfriend?" They giggled. "We had a bet about Charly," they told him.

"And what was the bet?" Charly asked, shrugging at Mason and making a face like *I don't know who they are*. She looked at his hands, then the messenger bag on his shoulder, then figured he'd checked her chocolate and caramel and pecan–coated popcorn with his luggage.

"That it was you. Your face and Annison—Oh. My.

God. Annison. Can you believe she's back after her sister Beyoncé'd her?—and some really fire-hot guy, and Sully, from *Nick*, of course. We can't believe they cancelled his show, but he's doing this now." The girls screamed.

"You know, we saw your commercial announcing the new series," the first girl said.

"Beyoncé'd her? What does that mean?" Charly had to ask.

"She overpowered her shine. Just like Beyoncé's career did to her sister's. Moved her outta the way like she'd never been there. I guess movie stars are bigger than television stars," one of the girls said. "Even with rollers in your hair, I could tell it was you!" another chimed in.

Charly's eyes bulged. "Oh no!" She touched her head and felt the rollers. She'd been in such a rush to get to the airport that she'd forgotten about them, and didn't know why no one had reminded her. She was going to kill Sully and Ramone, and especially the rest of Gossip Trinity who were supposed to be there to make sure she looked good, or so she thought. "Mason? Why didn't you say anything?"

Mason laughed. "And what was I supposed to do? I just got here, and you had them in your hair. I thought you knew. And besides, you're still beautiful."

"I also bet them that your show will be great!" the girl added, more than a little excited.

"Show? What show? You have a show, Charly?" Mason asked, proving that he clearly hadn't been paying attention the first time the girl had mentioned it. "You got cast?" He wore a look of pride.

Charly nodded. "Yes, but I just found out, like an hour ago. And it seems a commercial too. I don't know how they pulled that one off, because we didn't shoot a commercial together . . . not this cast. I haven't even met everyone yet."

One of the girls shrugged. "Putting a commercial together without everyone there is easy. People do that in the music industry all the time too. Anyway, my uncle does it. He's in California *and* he's a film editor. The commercial was like a series of you guys' clips merged together . . . not like a real *commercial* commercial," she informed, digging in her purse. She pulled out a permanent marker. "So, will you give us your autograph, and take a picture?"

Charly smiled, having her ah-ha moment, remembering what Sully had said about his media marketing father: *You'll see how cool soon.* Sully's dad must've had something to do with marketing the commercial, she assumed, reaching for the Sharpie the girl was handing her. "Sure," she began, then gritted her teeth when the girls whipped out their cell phones and started taking pictures of her in rollers. *Suck it up*, she told herself. *You wanted this, remember?*

Mason just stood to the side, wearing a million-dollar smile. "So, what does this mean? I can come to the taping of the show?" he asked as they made their way to get his luggage from off the conveyer belt after the girls had gone their separate ways.

Charly shrugged. "That would be so nice . . ." A partial lie began rolling off her tongue, but she stopped it. She couldn't be dishonest with him again; she'd grown up too much to continue to be childish. Her phone vibrated in her hand, and she looked at it. Mr. Day's assistant was texting in all caps. Charly needed to be back on the set ASAP. "But I'm not sure it'll be possible. I'll check though. If it's not, I'll make a way for you to come. You know how we do. But right now, we have to get to the studio."

3

Something about the taxi ride was off. Different. Charly looked over at Mason and wondered why he was so quiet. Ever since the airport and the screaming girls, he hadn't been his usual upbeat self. Then again, she told herself, he had just arrived. Maybe he was tired.

"You okay?" Charly asked, tilting her head in curiosity and admiring him at the same time. He was as fine as she remembered, and still made her stomach flutter.

He nodded. "The trip was long. I'm cool though," he replied.

Long? The flight couldn't have been more than two hours, and that was including boarding and deplaning the aircraft. Charly may not have flown a lot—okay, not at all—but she'd heard enough of her mother's complaints and had researched travel times online, so she knew. Still looking at him, she licked her lips, then shrugged.

Who was she to judge whether his day had been a lengthy one or not? She'd done plenty of traveling and had discovered short trips weren't always short. "Are you hungry? Because we can grab something to eat. I'm sure we have time."

Mason finally turned to face her. "Really?" His question said so much more than the one word that escaped his lips. His "really" was a mouthful of unspoken feelings, but his tone said it all. It was hopeful, as if he was happy that she hadn't forgotten about him.

Charly nodded. She had to be reading too much into his demeanor and question. There was no way Mason was acting funny. None. It wasn't like him to be, well, weird, she decided. "Yes. If you're hungry, we have time."

"Can you take us here first?" he said to the driver, scooting up to the edge of the backseat and pushing a small slip of paper through the small Plexiglas window that separated the back from the front. He'd moved so quickly, Charly was sure he hadn't had time to consider, let alone hear, what she'd begun to say.

Charly drew her brows together. "I meant we have time to eat at the *set*. There's food there. I saw the catering people setting up."

Mason pressed his lips together and gave her a look. "Well, what about my bags? I'm s'pose to just go to the studio with luggage?"

Charly laughed. Was he kidding? She'd traveled from Illinois to Michigan with suitcases, then from Michigan to Pennsylvania to New York with luggage and a puppy, so surely Mason couldn't have thought his baggage to be that big a deal. "Serious?" She shook her head. "I can put it in the dressing trailer if it'll make you feel better. It's really not a biggie." She smiled, then elbowed him. "Come on. Lighten up. You know you come first with me. Where's my Mason—the übercool Mason with the Brooklyn swag?" she teased, knowing he'd like being reminded of his New York roots. He'd been in Illinois for some time, and truly wasn't a fan of the small town his mother had "dislocated" them to, as he liked to say.

Mason nodded his head and smiled. Charly had broken his cool, and for a second his old self returned. He nudged her, then told the cabbie to forget the pit stop. His shoulders relaxed as he sat back. He took off his baseball hat, ran his hand over his waves, then quickly put it back on, adjusting it to the front. "Pardon me for girling out on you. I guess I'm just tired. You know us Brooklyn boys from the 'Bush aren't sensitive," he reminded her.

"Whatever!" She elbowed him again, and they both laughed. "You just want me all to yourself, Mr. Flatbush Brooklyn who traveled from Illinois to see me. Don't act otherwise." She bit her lip and went to reach for a lock of hair so she could twirl it, but her tresses weren't hanging over her shoulders as usual.

"Ahh. You forgot you got a headful of rollers. Didn't you, Ms. Superstar?" he teased, then became serious. "So you really got the series, huh? That's good stuff, Charly. I'm happy for you."

The cab pulled over a bit but was still blocking the cars behind it. Charly sat up and grabbed her purse, preparing to exit the taxi as car horns blared behind them.

"Uh . . . Charly?" Mason said, a pregnant pause between his words.

Charly opened her door, then looked over to him. His eyebrows were raised, half wiggling, half not, but definitely dancing and doing that thing that she loved so much. Then his expression went flat. "I uh . . ." He patted his pockets. "I'm kinda outta money until tomorrow morning because I sprung for my airline ticket at the last minute. My moms is going to wire me some—"

"It's cool," she assured him, digging into her pocket. She pulled out some cash, sticking the fare through the slot. "Keep the change," she told the driver. "Come on, Mason," she urged. "It's showtime. Let's see if I can keep you happy for me. I think a nice big meal will help."

"Uh . . . Charly?" he said, waiting for her to turn around.

"Yes?" She froze, not liking his tone.

"About the money . . . Well, I kinda didn't have enough to get you the popcorn either. Sorry about that."

Charly just nodded. She was disappointed, but it wasn't the end of the world. "No biggie, but you should've said something. I could have wired it to you."

"Let'sgolet'sgolet'sgo!" Ryan, the producer, was yelling again, this time running his words together, which signaled to Charly that they were behind. "Hey! You. Ms. Charly?" he boomed, walking her way with a clipboard tucked under his arm.

Charly froze. Mason stopped behind her, stepping on her heels. "Yes?" she asked, nervous.

"Day said you'd be back. I wasn't so sure though." He stopped short, grimacing. "I thought I sent you to hair and makeup. The makeup part I can see. But what the heck is going on with the rollers?" He looked around. "Hair! Someone get the Gossip Trinity out here, and tell 'em they have fifteen minutes to work out Charly's hair dilemma or I'm getting her a new stylist."

Charly threw Mason a look, then shrugged. Ryan was over the top and loud, and had now turned his attention away from her.

"Yo, what's he yelling at you for?" Mason asked, his expression even more twisted than Ryan's had been. "I don't appreciate him talking to you like that. Me and him need to talk," Mason snapped, then turned in the direction Ryan had taken. He took two steps before Charly stopped him.

A slight laugh sounded from behind, the delicious voice Charly remembered only too well and had memorized in a very short time. "He always yells. Seems he had a bit of a middle ear problem when he was just a kid, and hasn't been able to turn down his volume since. He doesn't mean any trouble by it. I don't think he's even aware of it," the voice said, walking in front of them. "Name's Liam, *Ms.* Charly St. James," he said, introducing himself to Charly. "So you're not a *he*," he said, referring to when he and Charly first met.

"Nope. I'm all *she*. Nice to meet you. Finally," Charly said, fighting a surfacing smile.

Liam moved over one step, then extended his hand to Mason. "Liam. You are?"

Mason puffed his chest a little. "Her man," he said. He turned to Charly. "Where's the trailer, baby? I need to put my things away."

Charly looked from Mason to Liam, then Liam to Mason. Her look told them both she was sorry. She thought Mason was being rude, and didn't understand it. Liam had been perfectly nice, and she hadn't flirted with him or anything. Had she? She shook off her questioning. There was no way Mason's actions were going to make her question herself. She hadn't done anything disrespectful, and she didn't even know who this Liam guy was except for his name and delicious accent, and now his supercute face; but Mason couldn't see her feelings and judgments. He had no right to act stupid or jealous.

"The trailer's back here. I'll show you," a female voice said.

Charly's head spun fast, and she locked eyes with Annison, who smiled at her. She wore what Charly assumed were her yoga clothes, which fit her like a second skin and showed all of her business. In her hand was a book that Charly couldn't see the title to. "Thank you, Annison, but no. I'll show him," she said, returning a forced smile. Annison's offering to show Mason where the trailers were had rattled her nerves, and now she kind of understood why Mason had reacted the way he had with Liam. She was perfectly comfortable in her own skin and didn't think any girl was better than her—even majorly famous ones like Annison. Still, there was something about a beautiful girl wanting to help her boyfriend that she didn't like. Charly shook her head, trying to shed the thoughts. Her being uncomfortable told her one of two things, and neither was good. Either there was something about her boyfriend she couldn't trust, or there was something about

Annison she shouldn't. Her instinct, though, she would trust. She'd bet everything on that, no matter what.

"Cool. I remember you," Mason said, smiling at Annison.

"Everybody does," Sully said from behind, slyly poking Charly in her back without being seen. "I'm Sully," he said, walking around and facing Mason. "And you must be the reason Charly broke her neck to get to the airport. Good to meet you, brah," he said, giving Mason a pound with his tattoo-covered fist.

Mason, to Charly's surprise, greeted Sully back. "Good meeting you, too," he said. "I remember your face too. You were on a kid's show or something, right?"

Sully nodded. "More like a teen show, but yeah."

Charly looked around for Liam while Mason and Sully talked. She wanted to try to apologize for the way her boyfriend was acting, but he was gone. For the life of her, she couldn't figure out why Mason didn't like Liam on sight but seemed okay with Sully. She shrugged. And people thought females were complicated?

"Oh, I didn't mean anything, Charly," Annison assured her, moving the book behind her back as if she were ashamed of having it. "I just figured I'd show your boyfriend where to go while you cleared things up with your dad."

Charly's eyes widened. "My dad?"

Sully nodded and adjusted his fisherman hat. "Yes. Your pop's here talking to Mr. Day. Seems he's a bit against you traveling. Something that should've been taken care of before the commercial was pieced together, if you ask me."

Charly shot Sully a don't-mess-with-me look, then rolled her eyes. He was right, but he didn't have to say anything.

Sully threw up his hands. "I got ya, Charly. I got ya. I know you're not to be played with. But don't shoot the messenger. It's nothing against your pops. I'm just saying."

Her heart dropped. She'd forgotten about her father and how protective he was. After he'd agreed to her doing the first show, which had been cancelled, she thought he'd be cool with the new one. She shrugged. How was she supposed to know he'd be wishy-washy? She'd just recently moved in with him after reuniting with him after eleven years, and found the relationship not to be as wonderful as she'd imagined. He was a military man who had military ways, and that meant his regimen was strict. He was all about education and hard work and educating oneself. Nothing else. He didn't see the need for the media or entertainment, and thought them both equally stupid. Television for him was the tell-a-lie-vision and history was his-story. Charly shrugged. "Thanks, Annison. If you don't mind showing him to the trailer, I'd appreciate it," she said, still hesitant about turning Mason over to one of the biggest female stars to ever hit the screen. She wasn't feeling too confident about leaving Mason, but she was happy that he didn't seem starstruck.

"And I'll show you where your father and Mr. Day are," Sully offered Charly. "This way."

She stood in the doorway, afraid to go in. Her father was in uniform, sitting in front of a desk. His foot was resting on his knee and his army-fatigue hat was on his lap. His expression, even from where she was standing, was serious. And so was Mr. Day's. "She's a child," her father was saying. "What kind of man would I be if I let my child travel across country? I let you talk me into letting her do the first show, but now this one?" He shook his head. "How do you expect me to let her participate in such . . . such . . . mess? Don't all these shows end up messy? I saw the music television series before—the ones where the kids moved from place to place. They were all messy, and the stars ended up in supermarket tabloids."

Mr. Day laughed, crossing his arms.

Oh no, Charly thought. *Don't do that*. She knew her dad could read Mr. Day and would take his arm-crossing as being defensive. She'd only been with her dad for a matter of weeks, but saw him study body and eye language. He was good at whatever he'd done for the military. So good, in fact, that they still contracted with him for certain operations after he was supposed to be retired, hence the uniform. He was currently involved in special ops.

Mr. Day looked her father dead in the eyes. "It's true, Mr. St. James. Most reality shows are a bit messy. Most of them. But not any show I've been in charge of." He uncrossed his arms. "You can check my credentials and they'll prove what I say is true." He grabbed a folder from a file, then handed it to her father. "Charly signed an agreement earlier, with the first set of contracts, and her mom has already given us written permission—that's why we're airing the commercial. Right, Charly?" Mr.

Day said, catching her spying from the door and waving her in.

Her father turned to her, and his look said she'd better not say a word. "Her mother? Well, she's a show all by herself," he admitted. "But that's a different story." He handed the folder back to Mr. Day. "Doesn't matter what Brigette signed. I have guardianship over Charly now."

Charly eased her way into the space between Mr. Day and her dad. She didn't know where to stand, so she thought it best to be between them so she wouldn't seem as if she was taking anyone's side. "Daddy?" she said, putting on a little girl voice, then thought better of it. If she acted like a child, he'd continue to treat her like one. She cleared her throat. "Dad, I'm your daughter, so you know I worked for this. I earned this. I traveled for this. And if it weren't for this . . . this television thing you're so against, you and I wouldn't be reunited." She hit him with a guilt trip, or at least hoped that she did.

Her father looked at her. Not a bit of guilt moved across his face, but his eyes softened. He blinked, then moved his gaze onto Mr. Day. "What's in this for Charly? I mean, what's in it for her later? Child stars come and go, then are left for the dogs because they lack education and get psychologically screwed up while you guys win. You get viewers, ratings, whatever, then move on to the next child star, the next show. In the meantime, she'll be putting food on your table and helping pay for your kid's tuition. What about her? What about her education and future?"

"Dad—" Charly began.

Her father held up a hand, silencing her.

Mr. Day smiled and nodded. "I understand where you're coming from. Trust me, she'll be compensated. She'll earn enough to cover her education and more."

Her father shook his head. "No. Trust isn't enough. I need black and white. Change her contract to include college tuition—undergrad and graduate school—and while you're at it, make sure to include a clause that guarantees the rest of her high school tuition is covered too." He gripped his hat, then nodded his head in acknowledgment. "Your studio is footing the bill for this online school she's in—summer classes and all—but I need to make sure that it's not a one-time deal. I mean, she does have to go to school online or have private tutors to finish, right? Especially if this reality show goes like you say it will."

Mr. Day grimaced and nodded.

"Well, you want my daughter to help you with your show. Told me the show couldn't survive without her just minutes before she came in. So, in my opinion, you have to help her with her future."

"Dad!" Charly protested. Her father was going to sink her ship before it arrived to carry her off to the life of stardom she'd dreamed of and had adventured for.

Her father held up one finger, and she quieted. There was no use fighting like she wanted to. She could challenge a map and travel across the states to get what and where she wanted, but there was no moving her father once his mind was made up, and she knew it. He was no Brigette.

Mr. Day scratched his head, then went and sat in front of his laptop. He clicked on the mouse and tapped on the keys for what seemed like forever. "Okay," he finally said. "I guess I can get accounting to work it into the budget since we're in contract negotiations."

Charly looked at Mr. Day like he'd grown a foot on his forehead, then cleared her throat until she got his attention. By now he surely had to know an "I guess" wouldn't be good enough for her father. "If it helps, I'll probably just attend a state college—not Ivy League or anything like that—so my tuition won't break the bank," Charly added, making a work-with-me face at him.

"Okay. Okay. You win, Mr. St. James. Send me a round figure that'll cover the tuitions, and we'll work it into the contract. Guaranteed." He stood and extended his hand.

Charly held her breath and prayed. With Brigette handling the contract with Mr. Day and the studio, she knew she could do anything she wanted as long as it equated to money her mother could spend. But her dad was different. He wasn't for sale, and her future wasn't up for negotiation. Either the studio would agree to his terms or talks would end. She wondered if Brigette's signature was enough. Did it really matter that her father now had custody if her mother had already given written permission for her to do a show? *Please, God. Please.* "He guaranteed," she whispered to her dad.

Her father stood and shook Mr. Day's hand. He nodded. "It was good doing business with you, sir," he said, then patted Charly on the head, placed his hat on his, and left.

Charly finally exhaled, and a huge smile spread her lips. She was going to be a star. She could feel it. "Yes," she exclaimed, following out behind her dad, then stopped.

Sully was waiting in the hall with his fisherman hat pulled down over his brows. He adjusted one of his earrings and stuck his other hand deeper into his pocket. He wore a suppressed grin that was steadily trying to spread into a full smile but only made it to a half sneer. "So, I take it your pops agreed to let you do the show?"

Charly nodded. "He did. I can hardly believe it, but he did. Mr. Day was fantastic about it too. He really helped." Her eyes widened, welcoming the face that now appeared behind Sully's. Liam was walking toward them.

Sully's lips finally spread and his top teeth gleamed. His version of a smile had won the battle and couldn't be suppressed anymore. "Great!"

Liam strolled up slowly, biting on his bottom lip. "So it's a yes now?" he asked as if he'd been there all along.

Sully's smile faded into a full sneer.

Liam patted Sully on the arm as he walked past. He grabbed Charly and pulled her in with a quick one-armed hug. Charly closed her eyes and took a whiff of the fabric softener smell of his shirt. "That's the best news I've had all summer," he said, moving the other arm from around his back and presenting her with flowers. "Nothing much . . . But I thought congratulations were in order."

Charly took the flowers and smiled. Who cared if they were mismatched and a couple of them were wilted. "Thank you! You're the best."

Liam's hands were now in his jeans pockets, and he

seemed to be blushing. "I *just* swiped them off a cart that was rolling by when I was walking over here. I guess someone's going to be disappointed their flowers didn't get delivered," he admitted, laughing. "Not a big deal, really. I just overheard your father talking to someone on his cell on his way out, and he mentioned letting you do the show. You know that without you it was dead, I suppose, at least for now. We needed two girls and two guys." He shrugged. "So that means with you doing it, we don't have to wait to find someone else. Trust me, the guys around here—me included—don't want someone else. She may not be as beautiful to look at."

Before Charly knew it, she'd wrapped her arms around him and hugged him tight. No one had ever brought her flowers before, and even if Liam had just swiped them, it didn't matter. It was the thought.

Three deliberate handclaps pulled her attention, and she released Liam. "Nice. Nice," Mr. Day was saying while approaching them. "That display. What chemistry. I think the viewers will eat it up. We're gonna have to play it up for the cameras."

Charly cringed. "There was no chemistry. It was only a friendly hug," she began, then turned to the side, hoping Sully would help her out. He'd somehow disappeared, but down the hall another pair of eyes was on her. She locked looks with a glaring and obviously rattled Mason, who was standing too far away to hear the conversation.

He threw up two fingers in the air, giving her the deuces-I'm-out sign, then turned his back on her and walked away.

Charly just stood there. She wanted to run after him but couldn't. She was at work, and there was no way she was going to risk losing the series because of Mason. She also wouldn't chance giving Mr. Day a reason to question if she was mature enough to handle such responsibility.

"Okay, it's all set then," Mr. Day was saying, backing up. He went into his office.

Liam smiled, then his eyes widened at something behind her back.

"What is it?" Charly asked, turning around. Her heart dropped, then skipped a little. Mason was walking toward them, and she couldn't read his expression. It was one she'd never seen before.

"Oh, I forgot to give you something," he was saying while approaching.

Her brows raised in question as he came nearer.

Mason walked between her and Liam, then reached out and pulled her to him. He held her tightly, then put his lips on hers before she knew it. It was a sweet kiss. "Congratulations, baby. I knew you could do it. Call me when you finish here."

4

Suitcases were strewn on the bed, clothes were everywhere, shoes polka-dotted the floor, and Marlow was sniffing the gadgets that were on top of the mattress. Charly sighed. It seemed as if she'd never be ready. She'd gone over her bulleted list of things to pack, and for some reason couldn't get it together. The list kept growing longer and longer by the hour. Worse still, she couldn't concentrate. The pressure was on. Annison was geared up and ready to roll, at least she'd said so each of the trillion times she'd texted. Sully was her newest fan according to his messages, though he'd accused her of falling for Liam's trick to get her attention, which she assumed was her accepting the swiped flowers. In addition, Stormy's tears had all but seeped through the lines of her texts, coupled with a "Do you have to go?" and "I'm going to miss you, Charly," as if they still lived in the same city.

Lola, her best friend in the whole world, had texted that she was pissed to the second degree and was divorcing Charly for abandoning her, then took it back after Charly promised that she could probably tag along on a couple of tapings because Annison was bringing a friend as well. She sighed, picking up her cell, seeing that the pressure of all pressures wasn't dissipating, namely Mason. She still hadn't seen him. After he'd left, his family had had some sort of emergency, so he was stuck babysitting at some relative's house in Brooklyn, and her father wouldn't let her leave the house. Now she couldn't get through to him, and it was killing her glee. She needed to see him before she left. She hoped he wasn't harboring bad feelings about Liam. Liam was cute and nice, but not for her. Her heart was for one guy and one guy only. Plus, Liam hadn't seemed interested. After the hug and stolen flowers, she hadn't heard from him. She tossed the phone onto the bedspread. She didn't have time to hunt down Mason, but she had his luggage. She'd texted him, and he replied that he couldn't get them before she left. Now her attitude was growing. If all of a sudden he financially had it like that to replace all the clothing he'd brought with him to New York, who was she to complain? She shook her head. She knew Mason didn't have money like that. He'd been waiting on his mother to wire him some cash; at least that's what he'd told her. But if he wanted to act like he didn't need his clothes, he could. She had her gear, and was looking at most of it in front of her.

"Whatever. Right, Marlow?" she said under her breath, trying to make herself angry with Mason. But the truth was, she was hurt. Hurt and disappointed that she wouldn't be able to see him before she left.

Her phone vibrated on top of the covers. She picked it up as quickly as she could, then smiled. He loved her. That's what his text said. Mason, like his usual self, had just made it all better, which is why she was crazy about him. A knock on her door pulled her attention. "Yes, Dad?"

The door opened. Her father walked in, eyeing the room from one wall to the next, then exhaled, looking at Marlow on top of the mattress. The untidiness from packing and her dog on the bed were probably getting to him. Since she'd been there she hadn't seen one thing out of order in the house, and had joked with him about being obsessive-compulsive, which, to her surprise, he admitted to. Everything had its place—one place—and that was all there was to it, he'd said with such authority that Charly knew he was forewarning her not to be messy. He pressed his lips together. "There's someone at the door for you."

Charly raised her brows. She wasn't expecting anyone, and knew it wasn't Mason. "Really?"

He nodded. "*Really*. And I don't know how I feel about it, Charly. It's a man."

Her eyebrows crunched together as she went temporarily dumb. She didn't know any men, at least not in New York. Her expression smoothed out when a clarifying thought surfaced. There could only be one man at the door. "You don't really think there's a problem with Mr. Day coming to get me, do you? I guess they decided against sending a car—"

He held up his hand, silencing her. "It's not Mr. Day. It's some dirty-looking man named Sully. Some man with a Southern accent and huge holes in his ears that I can see straight through. And there's someone else sitting in the car. A person I can't see."

Charly's heart raced and she laughed nervously. Her father's uncomfortable disposition had rubbed off on her, and now she was starting to question herself and her ears. Sully didn't have an accent. *Did he?* Like her bedroom, her thoughts were a mess. She looked at herself in the standing mirror across the room. Her appearance was even worse. "Sully's not a man, Dad. He's a teenager and my costar. And he doesn't have an accent."

Her father's uncomfortable expression twisted into something almost sinister. "Absolutely not. He's absolutely not your costar! You're not going on the road with all that . . . all that testosterone. I know what boys like him are up to. I was young once too."

"Dad, Mr. Day said girls and guys will be separate. Remember? Well, Sully's my costar who'll be traveling *separately*. The guys do the carpentry *and* have their own chaperones *and* stay in separate quarters. It's in the contract," she said, recovering. "Don't kill my dream, Dad. Please. Brigette's dream-massacring was enough. I worked hard for this. You of all people should be able to appreciate that," she said, hitting him with something she knew would flatter him and get under his skin and, hopefully, soften him up to the idea. "Can you please tell Sully that I'll be right out?" she asked when she saw him relax a little, but silently wondered who the mystery person in the car was.

*   *   *

When Charly exited the house, Sully jumped out of a new monster truck that definitely cost more than most people made in a year. He wore tattered jeans, a black T-shirt, rough-looking dreadlocks, nerdy spectacles, and a welcoming smile. He also had hair on his face. Charly's eyes zeroed in on him. He was haphazardly interesting looking, and the fact that he didn't seem to mind wearing weird-looking prescription glasses and hair that looked as if it'd been spun in a blender, made him kind of appealing. "Whaddya think? My new truck," he said, nodding.

"Hey . . . you, looking like a younger version of . . . I don't know? Rastafarian meets major nerd? I didn't know you wore glasses and dreads. The truck is nice. It fits you," she said, looking at the truck, and then at his hair. She wondered why she hadn't noticed how long it was before. It was too much to hide under a fisherman hat, and it was disarrayed, but the unkempt style looked good.

Sully ran his hand over his dreadlocks, then whisked it over the few hairs on his chin. "I'll take that as a compliment. I think the kinkiness will help on the road. No telling what kind of barbers—I mean, groomers—we'll have cutting us. It's better if all they have to do is line me up, and I may not let them do that." He shrugged. "Maybe I'll grow a beard to make Mr. Day lose it."

Charly shook her head. "Why would you do that, Sully?"

Sully laughed. "When I was doing that teen show, the dudes they had cutting us messed me up all the time. I'm not letting them do that again. TV can change you, if you're not careful. Like they didn't want me to pierce these like this." He pointed to the holes in his ears. "They said I looked like I was from an African village or a punk rock video. They don't get it. And this," he said, touching his hair. "If you like it . . ." He paused, then pulled at one of the locks. "Then that's a good sign. You don't seem like a fad person. I'm original, so I like original."

Charly smiled, now only feet from him. She appreciated the compliment. "So, why are you here?" she asked, not knowing what else to say. "I mean, what's up?" She didn't want to make him feel uncomfortable or unwanted.

He nodded toward the truck. "Thought I'd pick you up. I didn't see the need for some stranger in a limo to come get you, not when I'm going the same way and have this. So, here I am. Besides, limos are so boring, and who wants to be chauffeured and treated like a star, anyway?" he asked with a sarcastic grin, being silly.

Charly mockingly rolled her eyes. "I know, right. Who does that? Limos are so . . . everyday." They both laughed. "But I'm gonna need like fifteen, and, you know, Marlow, my dog, is coming with. Is that okay?" She started to walk away, then stopped. "Who's in there? My dad said you had someone with you?"

Sully nodded, then crouched down, petting Marlow. "Oh. Nobody. He probably saw all the bags of donation stuff I'm dropping off at the hospital. I was moving so fast, I tossed them in the front."

"Sully! That's sweet. Like books and stuff?" Charly asked.

Sully shook his head. "No! What kids want books when they're stuck in the hospital? I wouldn't. I got some autographed CDs, posters, video games, sports memorabilia, and some skateboards. The skateboards will be sent to shelters." He tapped his watch. "We have a schedule to keep, Charly. It's not a problem bringing Marlow along. There's not even a problem with the fifteen minutes, but we can't push for more than that. I have an errand too. While you're getting ready, I'll run up to the store, pick up a few things I know I forgot, put the donation bags in the back, then come back for you two," he said, scooping up Marlow in one arm, then standing. He ran his hand through Marlow's coat, handed her to Charly, then climbed into the truck.

Sully started his ride and pulled off. When he was finally out of sight, she breezed into the house like a hurricane to throw her stuff into the suitcases and convince her dad that going with Sully was okay. Fifteen minutes weren't nearly enough, but it was all she had.

The wind blew in through the windows, making her hair dance, and the music vibrated through the stereo system. Charly nodded and lip-synced B.o.B.'s lyrics while stealing glimpses of Sully, who was doing the same, except sound was coming out of his mouth. The more she was around him, the higher his friend-stock grew. Now he was funny, smart, sarcastic, and he could sing. Well, a little. But his okay-sounding voice was so much better than hers. He reached over and turned down the volume, stopping at a red stoplight and looking at her.

"What?" Charly asked, feeling a different vibe coming from Sully.

"*What?* That's how we talk to each other now?" he said with his sneer-like grin. Suddenly he paused his half smile, replacing it with a serious look. "So, about your problem?"

Charly watched as a couple of pedestrians passed the front of the truck while crossing the street. She looked at Sully. "Problem?" she asked, curious about which one he could've been referring to. "Which problem?"

He smiled at her, then winked, pressing his foot on the accelerator when the light changed to green. "You know, your *problem* problem. Your problem that weighs around one-eighty, is around my height, and likes to wear a Yankees cap. And runs away from what he thinks is competition. And you have another problem too."

Charly playfully punched him. "Mason's not a problem."

"Well, what is he then?" Sully threw her a quick look before turning his attention back on the road.

"He's my . . . well, he's my boyfriend," Charly said matter-of-factly. "And what other problem do I have?"

"Huh?" Sully hunched his shoulders and snickered. "Never mind the other problem. We'll see enough of him on the road," he said, letting Charly know he was talking about Liam. "But as I said: Mason, a problem. Your boyfriend, your problem. Trust me, if he doesn't change— if he doesn't realize that some things are good for the show, for your career, it's going to become a major problem. It's hard being on the road, and for some reason, boyfriends and girlfriends never get it." His eyes never left the traffic in front of them when he spoke. Charly just looked at him. The tone of his words said he was joking, but his look was serious. He'd become a friendly contradiction, and that worried her. She didn't know why though. Sully whipped the truck into a parking lot not far from the studio, then drove up ramp after ramp and level after level, finally parking in a numbered stall that she didn't think they'd fit into because the truck was so huge. "We're here," he said. "You take Marlow, and I'll take your bags."

Charly pressed her lips together. "What about your luggage?"

Sully flashed his version of a grin. "Oh, the only bags I have are for the sick and homeless, and my baggage for the show was picked up earlier."

"But I thought you were on your way here to the studio already . . . that picking me up was—"

"Optional?" he asked, moving his locks out of his face as he hopped out of the truck.

"Ha ha," Charly said sarcastically. She grabbed Marlow. "I was going to say *on your way*."

"Well, it was. Picking you up was on my way and optional. I had some stuff to handle out by your house, but I *wanted* to pick you up. Now, let's hurry to the studio before Mr. Day makes me lose it on him. If he says the wrong thing to me, you know I have to snap. It wouldn't be right if I didn't." He winked, and Charly couldn't tell if he was serious or not.

Charly followed Sully through the parking lot to the elevator. It took only seconds for it to open and them to hop on. Automatically she reached for the ground floor button, but Sully stopped her, then pressed twelve. Charly crinkled her brows, curious about where they were going. Though he smiled a lot and was sometimes painfully honest, something was off about him, and it wasn't just his dull coloring. He walked slowly and kind of weakly.

"C'mon," he said, pulling her bags behind him as he walked onto the twelfth floor, making a quick right.

"C'mon to where?" Charly asked, cradling Marlow and following.

"End of the hall," he said, throwing her a quick look. Charly's face must've told him that more information was needed because he nodded and snickered a little. "You're a lot like me, Charly. A tough one, and always questioning. We need to make a quick stop. No worries though. We'll be to the studio in no time. We're only a couple of blocks from there . . . and it's not like I'm going to try to kiss you or make a move on you," he assured her. "You're hot, but not my type." He laughed.

Charly followed, trusting him for whatever reason. Usually she'd have been more quizzical, more demanding that he answer her immediately. But with Sully she found herself very unquestioning, and she didn't want to fight it. Ever since she'd journeyed to New York and had been burned for being too trusting, her trust factor had been null and void, and she'd mistrusted just about everyone since then even when they didn't deserve it. Now it felt good to be at ease, and she hoped it wouldn't come back to bite her. She liked the brotherly feeling he gave; plus, she'd always wondered what it would be like to have one.

"Come in," he said, unlocking a door, then opening it for her.

When he pushed open the door she realized they were in an apartment building. "You live here?" she asked, entering and eyeing the place. Floor-to-ceiling windows lined one wall of the living room, and a surprisingly big kitchen opened onto it.

"Yes. This is home sweet home while I'm in New York. It was a part of my contract, so it's corporate's. I just live here for free, hopefully for a long time. My dad is supposed to be here with me, but he never is. He's either home in Texas or in Cali, where he does most of his business, but it's cool. I like being on my own." He nodded toward a sofa sectional. "You can have a seat or grab a bite from the kitchen. I just have to get a couple of things," he said, then headed down a short hallway.

Charly smiled, still taking in Sully's space. *It must be nice to have his own place*, she thought, making her way into the living room and taking a seat. She kept Marlow on her lap, not wanting to risk her making a potty puddle on the floor. They'd been cooped up in the truck for quite a while, so she knew Marlow might need to mark her territory. "We'll be leaving soon, Marlow. Then you can potty," she explained, looking into Marlow's eyes. She was sure her dog understood. Marlow seemed to have better comprehension than most people, as far as Charly was concerned.

"You like this?" Sully yelled. "Charly?" he called from wherever he was—his bedroom, she assumed. "Hey, Charly!"

Charly perked. Did he really expect her to come back there? she wondered. He'd just told her to take a seat.

"Charly?" he called again. Music suddenly filled the air. It was a song she'd never heard, but it was nice.

"Sounds good," she answered. "Yes," she said louder. "It's really hot. The bass line is heavy," she admitted, rocking her body to the rhythm, then stopped. Her phone was vibrating in her pocket, stealing her attention. She took out her cell, then froze for a second. Mason's name was on the screen. Her focus shifted left, then right, looking for Sully and a place she could safely answer the phone without giving away her whereabouts. He'd already encountered one bad costar situation; she didn't want him to be uneasy about her being at Sully's apartment. "There," she mumbled to Marlow, noticing a terrace outside, just off the kitchen. In seconds she was through the kitchen, opening the glass door and making her way out to answer his call.

"What's up, baby?" Mason asked with a smile in his voice.

"You," Charly replied, looking over the edge of the patio before taking a seat on one of the chairs. The wind whipped past her lips and into the phone, then horns blared, their sounds making their way all the way up to the twelfth floor.

"What's all that noise? You outside?" Mason asked.

"Okay, Charly," Sully said from behind, standing at the doorway to the terrace. "I got everything I need from my bedroom. I'm ready when you are."

Charly swallowed. She hadn't heard Sully open the door, and hoped Mason didn't hear him.

"*Bedroom?* Who's that, Charly?"

"Um . . ." she replied, grasping at the air for acceptable and believable answers to Mason's questions. "Well—"

"You ready?" Sully asked, stepping all the way out onto the terrace, then grimacing. His face said he didn't realize she was on the phone. "Sorry," he mumbled, backtracking inside.

Mason's laugh was low and filled with disgust as it traveled from his phone to her ear. "Oh. Word? I gotcha. You not answering my question just told me everything I need to know. Enjoy hanging out with your new boyfriend, or whatever he is. I guess it was what it was the other day, huh?"

The line went dead.

5

THE EXTREME DREAM TEAM
SCHEDULED Show 1 itinerary

Recipient information:

Home fire victim
HARGROVES, ELISA
Fourteen-year-old female
Valedictorian, class president
Founder of RMAA (Raising Money & Awareness) for
the Homeless
EXTREME DREAM TEAM Mission: Design and build
Elisa a new bedroom and office for RMAA.
> **Charly's duties:** Assist Annison with design. Mediate between design (Annison) & carpentry (Liam).
> Communicate with and be responsible for recipient
> being away from location.

Locale: CHICAGO, ILLINOIS

* * *

The itinerary shook in her hands before falling to the dressing room floor. Charly's head almost exploded as her eyes zeroed in on the destination. No way, she mumbled, sure that her vision was deceiving her. Mr. Day couldn't have possibly thought it was okay to send her back to where she'd escaped from, not after she'd told him her story when they first met. Her mother had mistreated and stolen from her—her money and her dreams— and had made Charly her personal Cinderella, who she was determined to turn into a factory worker. Never mind college or stardom. Never mind love or food or stability. Charly had been deprived of all of those; then she took her life into her own hands and hopped on a bus to make a getaway to save her future before her mom could finish massacring her hopes. "No, not there again." She grabbed both sides of her head, pressing on her temples. A headache was throbbing its way into a life-altering migraine, clearly out to match her upcoming trip. "Chicago, Marlow. You've never been there," she said to her beloved pooch, who stood faithfully at her feet, looking up at Charly like she understood her master's pain.

"Chicago. Cool, huh?" Annison asked, popping up out of nowhere. Charly blinked slowly, then noticed a little crayon-red poodle in Annison's hands that was no bigger than a fleeting thought. "This is Doll," Annison said, holding up the tiny dog that looked like she'd been dipped in paint. "My companion who's coming with me on the road and now Marlow's friend too. And isn't she pretty? The people we rescued her from had her dyed!" She squealed her words like a cheerleader, then followed with, "*The Extreme Dream Team*'s first mission—starring Annison and Charly—saving extreme do-gooder Elisa's day and bedroom. Yay!"

Charly looked at the bright red dog, wondering if the dye chemicals would harm her, then thought better of it. Annison was very sweet to have rescued the poor thing. She brightened. Maybe the trip back to Chicago wouldn't be so bad. She'd left Illinois just another teenager on a dream mission, but would be returning as the costar with Annison—a real certified star who'd actually earned her star stripes and status, and wasn't just another falling, one-named idol who'd managed gobs of media attention for less than starlike reasons. Namely, the hoteliers' and famous attorneys' kids of the Hollywood and Hollyhood worlds—the Parises and Kims. No, Charly was being ushered in by an award-winning actor. An actor who cared, and that made all the difference. Not to mention, Marlow had a playmate in Doll. "Yes, it's cool," Charly said, convincing them both. "And I'm ready," *since you asked like a kazillion times via text*, she wanted to add but didn't. This time around would be great, and she wouldn't let a bad attitude change it.

Annison wrapped one arm around Charly in a half hug. "I'm excited, Charls. It's going to be nice to have someone to help . . . you know, with the show," she said, her eyes were void of feeling again, like someone had just died. She pasted on another phony smile. "I feel good about this, Charls," she cut Charly's name in half for the second time, making Charly wince. It was bad enough people mistook her name for a guy's almost all the time, but to have it shortened to Charls—which was way too similar to Charles—made it worse.

"Just call me Charly, Annison. Just *Charly*, and nothing else. '*Kay?*" she said with emphasis, trying to be as friendly as she could, patting Annison's back. But she knew the words came out raw, without a hint of easiness. She didn't like *Charls*. Point blank and period, and she wouldn't pretend to. "And I'm excited too," she admitted, finally shaking the ill feelings about traveling back to her hometown. "So excited." She stepped back, grinning. "So we're leaving in a few. I can't wait to see our bus." She brightened even more when Liam, Mr. Beautiful-Accent Guy himself, walked into the dressing room after announcing himself with a knock.

"Our bus . . ." Annison nodded very slowly. Her eyes widened at the sight of Liam. "Charls, could you be a doll and hold Doll for me?" Her laugh was slow and deliberate as she bobbed her head, the laugh sounding more like *uh-huh, uh-huh* than genuine laughter.

"Charly, Annison. *Charly*. Remember?" Charly corrected, rolling her eyes.

Annison just kept on talking as if Charly hadn't spoken. "Pun intended. Doll and doll, get it? Hold her for me, please. I just gotta go take care of something really quick," she said, still ignoring Charly's request to call her Charly. "Liam, are you coming with?"

Liam looked at his phone in his hand, which had begun to vibrate. He shook his head. "No, but I do have to run. I just wanted to wish you girls luck, and let you know I look forward to working with you," he said, making his way past them both.

Charly just looked at him with wide eyes. He was so gorgeous she couldn't help staring at him, but she tried the best she could. The last thing she wanted was for him to feel like she was stalking him. Suddenly he turned and winked, then disappeared out the trailer's door. Charly gasped. Had he really winked at her, or had she imagined it? She shook her head, then heard Annison clearing her throat. "Oh," Charly said, taking Doll and carefully balancing her in her arms like a newborn baby. The dog was so tiny she felt as if she'd break if not handled with the utmost care. "How old is she?" she asked Annison, who'd begun to make her way toward the door until something more important snatched her attention—her reflection in a mirror hanging on the wall. She stopped then centered herself in front of it, whipped out a lip-gloss tube, then glossed her lips. She fixed her hair next.

Sully walked in with a scowl on his face and a different ring through his eyebrow. "Hey, what's up?" he asked, his tone contradicting his glare. He threw an iffy glance back Liam's way, and Charly figured out what—rather, *who*—Sully's underlying problem was.

"Sully, you're a scrooge," Charly said, then gave him a knowing look. "Don't be so transparent," she advised, then turned her attention. "So, Annison. How old is Doll?" she repeated.

Annison shrugged, then looked over her shoulder at Charly. "A year or so, I think, but I can't be sure since Doll's a rescue. I'd never *buy* a puppy—not when so many need homes." She smiled, then walked past Sully on her way out the door.

Sully rolled his eyes mockingly. "Yeah, right," he said,

making his way over to Charly. "She'd buy anything—rather, she'd have her handlers buy anything—if it made her look better, including the title of dog rescuer."

Charly wasn't going to touch his accusation. For some reason, Sully didn't seem like too much of a fan of Annison's, and if she remembered correctly, her stylist team, especially Ramone, didn't seem like a cheerleader for Charly's costar either. She shrugged. Everybody wouldn't like everybody; that was the way of the world. But she wasn't here to get caught up in other people's messes. She just wouldn't. Who needed real-life drama when they were after television drama? Not her. "What's up, Sully? You ready to hit the road?"

He shrugged. "I don't know. Ready might not be the right word, but I'm going if that's what you're asking. Work is work, right?" He tilted his head toward the door. "And working with her is going to be overtime."

Charly couldn't take it. She'd just told herself not to meddle, but Sully was making it incredibly hard. "So what's the deal, Sully? Do you just not like everyone?"

Sully reared back his head, then scooped up Marlow from the floor, where she'd begun to whine. "I never said I didn't like Annison."

Charly laughed because Sully had just told on himself. She'd never accused him of not liking anyone by name. "So it's just Annison you don't like?"

He laughed, petting Marlow. "Charly, you got me all wrong. Believe it or not, I do like Annison. I may not always like to be around her or agree with her, but I can deal with her. She's unhappy, unpleasant, insecure and sometimes she's even underhanded, but at least she doesn't hide it. I can deal with anyone who's honest about who they are. But the other one—the dude from "across the pond"—he's a different story. He's fiction. I don't do make-believe very well. It goes against my beliefs."

Charly gasped. So he could also see that Annison wasn't happy. But he was also unpleasant, just like he was pessimistic and unfriendly and maybe even a little jealous, which was why he wasn't a favorite of many on the set, she decided. But he was cool with her, and that's all that mattered. She nodded, agreeing with him. "I'm like that too, Sully. As long as I know who someone is, I can deal with them too." She cradled Doll. "And I'm ready to hit the road and deal with the show," she said, trying to lighten the mood. "So, again, are you ready? To work?" she added.

"Yes, and it seems Marlow is too. I think she's sad that you're holding another dog." He turned his body sideways, sticking his rear her way. "There's a note for you in my pocket," he explained.

Charly shifted Doll to one arm and took the note.

To: Ms. Charly St. James (of *The Extreme Dream Team* cast)
From: Lola
Message: See you in the Chi!!!

Charly crinkled her nose. How did Lola know her itinerary just minutes after she'd found out herself? "Mr. Day, I assume?" she said aloud.

Sully shrugged. "I got that from one of the studio runners who saw me and stopped me on my way here."

Charly raised her brows, indicating she didn't know what a studio runner was. "You know, one of the people who run around the studio, and we don't quite know what they do or who they are. Pay attention. There are a lot of them—the ones who you don't really *really* know who they are, and not necessarily studio runners either, and you know who I'm talking about too. Be careful with *him*. Now let's switch pups. I'll give Annison's to her people."

"Okay. You got it, Sully. I'm paying attention," she said to appease him and to acknowledge his warning about Liam. She didn't feel the same way about Liam as Sully. To her, Liam seemed genuine, but she decided not to get into that with Sully. "Here." She swapped out Doll for Marlow, then paused.

Sully began to walk away, holding Doll. "Well, c'mon, Charly. It's time to go. The tour bus awaits."

It wasn't Greyhound or any other type of bus she'd ever seen, Charly noted, holding Marlow. The tour bus was the Air Force One of all passenger carriers on the road with wheels and axles, she decided as soon as she boarded. Two plush leather loveseats and chairs, mounted flat-screen televisions, and a mini gourmet kitchen she could see tucked in the back through theater-like curtains, met her eyes and spread her lips into a smile. Charly's eyes darted back and forth, looking for where she was to lay her head. The space was elegant, not palatial, so there were no designated bedrooms.

"Back there, through the curtains, is what you're looking for." Sully's deep voice came from behind, almost making her jump out of her skin. Before she'd boarded the bus, Sully had walked to the bus behind the one she was on, so she didn't expect to see or hear him until they reached Illinois.

Charly turned, drawing her brows together.

Sully pointed his tattoo-covered hand. "You're looking for your bunk, right? Well, you can't see it from here. The curtains are hiding them, but trust me, they're there. Two on each wall—two too-narrow ones, if you ask me. You'd think the studio would've done better, with all the money we're going to make 'em."

Charly stopped herself from rolling her eyes at Sully's unfounded complaint. How was the studio supposed to do better, widen the bus? "Impossible," she muttered as her shoulders relaxed. At least she'd be comfortable. With four bunks, two on either side, she and Annison and their dogs would have plenty of room. "Cool. That gives me and Marlow our own bunks. I guess Annison and Doll have theirs too. I wonder if Annison will want a particular side."

Sully made something like a snorting noise, then moved past her. Charly noticed his shoulders trembling with silent laughter, and didn't see what was so funny. Then she noticed he had a leather travel bag in his hand. A big one, she noted, watching him walk toward the back, then lift the oversized case and place it on what she assumed was one of the bunks. "Do you want top or bottom?" he asked, loud enough for her to hear.

"Excuse me?" she asked, finally setting Marlow on the floor and watching her race around in small circles.

Charly turned her attention back to Sully. "Aren't you on the other bus, the *boys'* bus?"

He pulled back the curtain a bit, enough for her to see his face. "Yes, Charly. I am." He forced a smile, then purposely cringed. "I'm not sure if you know it or not, but *this* is the other bus."

Charly didn't understand. She was sure that males traveled separate from females, and had been assured by Mr. Day that she and Annison would be together. "You sure? I'm almost certain that costars bus with costars. So that means me and Annison and you and . . . Liam?"

"Yes, Liam," Sully said, approaching her. "It's okay to say his name. I see how you look at him," he teased. "But yes, that's my costar—no, I take that back. I'm *his* costar. *Costar* is supposed to mean we're equal, but he's like huge in England—like *Idol* huge, bigger than me and my teen Nick show. Anyway, that's who we're waiting on. I'm sure I would text him to hurry—okay, actually I wouldn't. I don't talk to him unless I'm forced to—but even if I was willing, my cell only makes and accepts calls. It doesn't text or go online. I don't believe in all this technology—it's an interruption of life." He looked at his watch. "I think English Pretty Boy Floyd's helping Annison and her crew on *the main* bus. The real limo of the highways."

Charly shook her head. Nothing made sense. She took her phone from her pocket to see that her battery was almost dead.

Sully continued. "Really? I guess you don't know the real deal about this series. Annison and Liam are the costars; we're their sidekicks. They can dress it up and call us costars if they want; it isn't true though. She gets her own bus, and only she and her assistants ride in her motor limo. We, on the other hand, get to ride in our motor coach."

Now Charly was confused. "I thought you said they—Annison and Liam—are the stars. What bus does he ride in?"

Sully laughed. "He doesn't. He flies everywhere in a jet. Period."

"Miss? Sir? Can I get either one of you anything? Perhaps something for the puppy?" a raspy voice interrupted.

Charly turned around just as she'd reached the bunks—the tiny bunks that couldn't have been more than three feet wide and six feet long—and laid eyes on a tall, burly boy whose hair was missing. All of it. From where she stood, she didn't see hair or eyebrows, and she assumed his eyelashes weren't there either. She spotted an outlet next to the bunks and plugged in her phone.

Sully laughed. "Good one," he said to the guy. "Perhaps! Ha!" He was amused. "You sound just like you're from across the pond."

"Right?" the guy said to Sully. "Anyways, we're here!" He turned his attention to Charly. "I'm Eight," he said, then lifted his hands, showing off a blur of red fuzz. "Oh, and how could I forget the most important person on this bus, Annison's Doll?" He sneered. "She's all yours, Charly."

Charly drew her brows together. What on earth was this guy talking about? "Sorry?"

He laughed. "My name's Eight. Really. And don't laugh

because it's not funny. Before you ask, let me run the math for you. I was born August eighth at eight-oh-eight in nineteen eighty-eight. And Doll's all yours."

Charly nodded, taking in his answer. It was the most ridiculous thing she'd ever heard, but all the eights made sense, so if his mother wanted to name him after numbers, what business was it of hers?

Sully walked up to her and put his hand on her back, then walked to the sitting area. "He's telling the truth, Charly. Eight's a good guy. He's with me. Long story."

"Oh, and by the way, I also serve as chaperone. You didn't expect the studio to let a bus full of teens travel without supervision," Eight said.

Charly's smile faded behind Eight's back. She didn't like being babysat, but knew there had to be some sort of rules or laws against a bus full of teenagers traveling across country without an adult overseeing them. She reared back her head in surprise, wondering what else she didn't know about. "Where do you sleep?" she asked before she could stop herself.

Eight smiled and pointed to the back. "There's a fold-out, kinda like an old-school Murphy bed. It's out of your way, so no need to worry about that. But you do need to worry about Doll. She's all yours," he said again, then looked down at Marlow, who ran in quick circles on the floor at Eight's feet, looking anxious for him to put Doll down. Sully, now sitting in one of the leather chairs, crossed his leg over his knee like Charly's dad would while reading a magazine, and laughed.

Charly's eyes bulged. She pointed to her chest. "Me? Whadda ya mean, she's all mine?"

Eight put Doll down, then made his way back to her. "Per Annison, Doll is supposed to be with you and Marlow."

Charly put her index finger to her lips. "Well, let me think about that for a second," she said, pausing. "Nope! That's not going to happen. I'm just going to take Doll back to her owner."

"Ready? Let's hit the road, kids!" the bus driver said, suddenly in his seat. He closed the doors, revved the engine, and pulled off before Charly could get in another word.

6

Charly turned a fraction of an inch, then moved again, thinking the expression *tossing and turning* couldn't have come from someone who'd ridden a tour bus, at least not the one she was on. She punched her pillow to soften it, then folded her midsection until it curved in. Doll and Marlow had made themselves comfortable next to her navel and were now slumbering like infants against her stomach. Charly rolled her eyes. It was a shame that two little dogs, sleeping so soundly, could prevent her from doing so. Because she couldn't straighten out, she couldn't rest. She exhaled long and loud, releasing her frustration.

"Charly, you good down there?" Sully asked, his deep voice coming from the top bunk across from hers.

Charly reached out and pulled back the curtain that sealed off her bunk from the others. "Yes. It's just hard to sleep with these two crowding me, and because of the newness of it all."

"Yo, meet me in the back to grab a quick bite," Sully half spoke, half whispered, his voice too deep to fully whisper. "I'm starving."

She heard Sully moving around on his bunk, then his feet thumped on the floor. With a lot of effort, she managed to worm her way around Marlow and Doll without waking them, careful not to bang her head on the top bunk, which was barely three feet above hers. She slid open the curtain, but not all the way. She didn't want the light to hit the pups and wake them. Her feet connected with the cold floor, and the coolness traveled from her soles to her head. "Great," she mumbled, walking the few feet to the kitchen area to meet Sully. "Now I'm cold too," she complained, then reminded herself that she wanted all this. She desired fame, so she had to take everything that went with achieving it.

She'd taken only seven steps when she bumped into Sully's rear. "Sorry," she apologized, squinting her eyes in the barely lit area.

"No problem. You can run into me anytime. Any time at all," he teased. He was bent over with his head in the refrigerator. "Here," he said, passing back pita bread, a huge bag of potatoes, and a container of hummus.

Trying to balance the pita bread and hummus, the bag of potatoes started to slip from her grasp. "No . . ." she sang loudly, trying to catch it before it hit the floor or her bare foot. The last thing she needed was ten pounds of spuds hurting her before the show had even started.

"Ssh," Sully whispered, then stood, pointing to a small area off the tiny kitchen. "Eight's knocked out." He reached for the potatoes. "We're not having these, Charly. I just needed you to hold them until I got the turkey from behind the hummus. They were in the way."

Charly followed his finger and, sure enough, Eight was asleep on a bed that unfolded from the wall and couldn't have been any larger than her own. Half of it was exposed, and the other part was hidden behind the sink area. Charly guessed Eight had to climb in to lie down, but obviously wasn't uncomfortable. His mouth was hanging open, and he was snoring ever so slightly.

Suddenly things changed. Bright light assaulted her eyes. People, at least two, appeared out of nowhere. A camera was stuck in her face. A microphone on a long pole was over her head. Gobs of wires seemed to be everywhere.

"Oh. What the—?" Sully shouted.

"Duck!" Charly said.

Sully, with two plates and jar of mayo in his hands, ducked and banged his head on the counter. "Ow. That's gonna leave a knot on my forehead."

Charly grimaced. "I didn't literally mean duck, Sully. I was saying to *say* duck. Duck, you know, so you don't use the *f* word. Say duck instead of cursing. Got it?"

The cameraman rolled his finger in a circle, urging them to keep going. "We're filming," he mouthed.

"Duh, like we couldn't tell," Sully said sarcastically, standing and pressing a canister to his head. "The pressure should help stop it from knotting up so big," he explained, looking at Charly, then he turned his attention to the men. "When did you guys get on this bus?" he asked, not looking half as surprised as Charly.

Charly looked from Sully to the cameraman to the guy holding the boom mic over their heads.

The cameraman shook his head. Microphone-man leaned the mic against the wall, took out a notepad from his back pocket, then began to scribble on it.

FILMING <u>EVERYTHING</u>! DESTINATION & THE ROAD. IT'S <u>ALL</u> REALITY.

He flipped the page and began scribbling again.

GOT ON WHEN YOU WERE SLEEPING. KEEP GOING. BE NATURAL. WE'RE TAPING!!!

Charly nodded. So now she was supposed to pretend the extra passengers weren't on the bus, grab a bite with Sully, and be natural? Sure. She could do that, she told herself. She had to. Never mind that she was dog-tired and tired because of the dogs. Who cared that she probably looked something like a raccoon from lack of sleep and was wearing her pajamas. "So . . . ," she began. "What are we eating?" she asked Sully, trying to be as natural as she could. "Hummus or turkey?"

The bus jerked, followed by a loud mechanical yawn. Charly's body flew to the side, bumping the wall, then bounced, hitting Sully. The camera shifted on the man's shoulder before falling. In one quick swoop, he dove to the floor and caught the camera before it hit. The bus yawned again, then the motor died. The lights flickered off, then on, then off again.

"Serious?" Charly yelled. "Somebody tell me this is a joke."

Noises rattled from the front of the bus. Eight stirred from his recess in the wall. A *tha-thump* could be heard from the bunk area, followed by Eight hissing a few curses about banging his head. Marlow and Doll started to whine.

"No, I can't lie to you," Sully said. "This is not a joke."

Charly turned in the dimness, barely able to see the cameraman. The light filtering in from outside allowed her to see his silhouette. "Does that thing have battery power at all?"

He nodded.

"Don't nod. Talk! We're not taping, so what's the big deal?" Charly's hands were on her hips.

"Of course it has batteries," Sully answered for the cameraman.

"So please turn on the light. The camera has a light— you just blinded us with it, so I know it's there," Charly urged.

With only one click, Charly was almost blind again from all the wattage. "Good," she said. "Follow me." Barefoot, she pivoted, walking toward the front of the bus, then stopped at her bunk. "I just need to get Marlow and Doll to make sure they're okay. Plus, by now I know they have to go potty. No sense in allowing them to make un-necessary doggy deposits on my bunk." She drew back the curtain, took out Marlow and set her on the floor, then Doll. "Mr. Driver! Mr. Driver! Please show me where the motor is," she said, making her way to the front door. "I didn't come all this way to fail. There's a girl in Chicago who needs us, and we're going to help her. Period!"

Charly learned two important things about the driver. First, his name was Driver. "Just Driver," he'd informed her after she introduced herself and then asked for a flashlight so she could tinker with the motor. Second, Driver didn't let anyone touch his bus. "Period. Not a soul touches the soul of this here bus—and the engine is the soul. Sorry, Charly." He'd been final with his words.

Charly stood on the side of the road, piecing it all together. This was a show—a series on a major network—so there had to be a backup plan. There were, after all, other buses. Annison had one, and she was sure there was another for equipment and other things necessary for filming.

Sully stomped off the bus, cursing. He wrapped his fingers around his dreadlocks and tied them into a knot. He yawned and stretched, then slipped on his sneakers. "So when does the cavalry arrive?" He directed his question to Eight, who was now leaning against the bus.

Eight shrugged, then held his phone in the air. "No reception."

Charly's head almost fell off. "Whaddya mean, no reception? There has to be a way to communicate. You mean the bus's walkie-talkie-whatchamajig doesn't work out here? There's no generator?"

Eight shook his head. "Not without power. And there's

no power. Driver said the outlets stopped working, which means those of us who had our phones plugged in to charge . . . well, guess what?"

Charly smirked. "They weren't charging. So there's nothing?" She was exasperated. She'd suffered enough of the blues while traveling from Illinois to New York to know that the feeling in her gut was never wrong. And her instinct and intuition told her she'd have to make a way out of no way again: this time from wherever they were now, to Illinois.

"Let me check with the crew," Sully said, sidestepping the cameraman, whose camera was still lighting the way for Charly. "Okay, let me check with the boom guy." He disappeared back onto the bus.

Charly walked over to Driver. "Do you know where we are?"

Driver smiled, nodding. "Sure I do. We're in the middle of nowhere, about two hours from lost." He laughed quietly, embarrassed. "Just joking, Charly. Really, I can't tell you without the right map, and I'm afraid I left it at home. I was using the GPS on my phone to bypass the interstate, which I hate traveling. I was trying to get us there faster, but please don't tell anyone. I'll lose my job."

"Don't tell anyone? We're lost! And you don't want me to tell—"

Driver held up his hand. "Please, Charly. You're young. You wouldn't understand if I told you."

Charly crossed her arms. "You better make me understand, Driver. Either that or I'm tinkering with the engine."

Driver stiffened. "Not the engine." He leaned toward her. "My wife . . ."

Charly rolled her eyes, preparing for Driver's pitiful story of his wife dying or leaving him, some fictionalized story she was sure he'd use on her to persuade her not to tell.

"Yes, that Bridgette, she's always gambling. Now she done went and gambled the mortgage. I was so mad, I took this job to get me out of there. I usually drive locally, I don't normally drive long distance, unless I have to."

The mention of Bridgette and her gambling snatched away Charly's anger with Driver for not having the proper map. Her mother's name was Brigette, probably spelled different than Driver's wife, but that was enough to make Charly sympathize. Her mother was a gambler too, and had gambled away Charly's hard-earned money, which had fueled Charly's decision to go to New York to pursue her dream. She shook her head. Now because of the Brigettes she was stuck again.

"I think we're somewhere in Ohio," Driver said. "The sign said so a ways back."

Charly exhaled, then began to pace. She had to think of something to do. There had to be a way to get to Chicago.

"Boom-guy says no generator, and no generator means no power," Sully said, stepping off the bus. "Now ain't this some . . . ?"

"I have some," Eight said, his voice booming from inside the bus. "I have an extra battery—it has some juice in it, but not much. And my Wi-Fi isn't working. We can't go online," he said, running out and tripping. Muffled curses came from his mouth. "And no one's answering at the studio. Does anyone have Mr. Day's direct number or the number of someone on Annison's bus?" he asked, finally stepping onto the ground.

Everyone looked around at everyone else. A bunch of *not me*s filled the air.

"The only numbers I know off top are my parents," Sully said, then shrugged. "But they're in India or China by now. They're on vacation. Then again, they may be in Texas or California and just not answering. It wouldn't be a first." He spat on the ground, shaking his head.

He clearly had issues with his parents, at least his father, Charly thought, then scratched her head. "I can call my sister. I can't forget her number—we're only one digit off from each other."

Before Charly knew it, she had Stormy and Lola on the line. She was walking and pacing, easing farther away from the bus to keep the phone's signal strong. Sully was on her heels, listening and watching over her. He needed to be sure she was okay, he'd said.

"You need to find out where you are so I can tell you where to go," Lola said.

Charly rolled her eyes. "Lola, that's the problem. That's why I'm calling. We're lost!" she snapped.

"Charly. Charly, calm down," Stormy advised. "Lola, you know they're lost. We established that as soon as we got on the phone. My sister barely has any light besides the stars in the sky, so how's she supposed to see down the street?" Stormy offered, explaining for her sister.

"Yes!" Lola screamed through the line. "That's it. Hold on one sec, I'm calling Smax."

"Smax? I don't need Smax. I need a tow truck!" Charly yelled.

"Okay. So I can call a towing service. But where should I tell them to go if you don't know where you are?" Lola pointed out.

"Good point," Stormy said.

"Okay. Smax it is!" Lola said, then clicked over.

Charly crinkled her brows. Why on earth was Lola calling Charly's old boss and Lola's rumored biological father, Smax? Smax wasn't a driver or well traveled. He didn't even know how to use a computer. He was old-school, and right now Charly missed him and his wife, Bathsheba, like crazy. She would've loved to have been with them in the safety of their rib spot, rather than out here in the middle of nowhere.

Lola clicked back in. "One sec. I'm calling Doc," she said, then clicked off again.

"Doc?" Stormy asked.

Charly nodded her head as if Stormy could see her. "Yes. Dr. Deveraux El. You may've seen him at Smax's. He's the one who sits at the bar studying history, the zodiac, maps. Lola must've gotten his number from Smax. But why is she calling him?" Charly wondered aloud.

"Oh yes. Him. I met him, Charly. He's the one who told me I didn't have a name. He said people were given titles, not names. And names are only for birth certificates or something like that."

Charly laughed. Yes, her sister had met Dr. Deveraux El.

"Charly? Stormy?" Lola asked, finally back on the line. "I have Doc on the phone."

"Charly? My dear sister, Charly. Can you tell me, do

you know where Ursa Minor is in the sky? If we can find that, I can get you to your destination," Dr. Deveraux said as if his question was as simple as *Have you ever drunk water?*

"Ursa Minor?" Charly asked.

"Yes. You know, Polaris? Ursa Minor, Ursa Major . . . Great Bear and Little Bear? The tip of Ursa Minor is Polaris, and Polaris doesn't move; it guides," Dr. Deveraux explained.

Charly looked left, then right. The answer didn't come from anyone in either direction, and it certainly wasn't coming from her head.

"Oh, you mean the North Star?" Stormy's voice chimed in.

"Exactly, Sister Stormy," Dr. Deveraux praised. "If we can help Charly read that . . . if she finds the North Star, then she'll know every other direction."

Great. Now I gotta be Harriet Tubman . . .

7

The phone had died. The cell she'd borrowed from Eight had keeled over in her hand, screaming from too much North Star information and not enough battery juice. Charly looked at the small screen and shrugged. Okay, so it hadn't folded over and cried out, but she certainly felt like hollering at the top of her lungs after talking to Stormy and Dr. Deveraux about the Ursas, which she'd lied about spotting. Yes, she knew where they were now, had memorized everything she could about Polaris and the dippers and bears, so she didn't see the sense of dragging out the conversation, especially when she overheard Driver saying something about progress and getting off the side of the road soon.

Eight walked up to her. "You good?" he asked. His hand was extended.

Charly put the dead phone on his palm. "Sorry. It died before I finished talking." She looked around, searching for Sully's silhouette in the darkness. Somehow it seemed to have grown darker since she'd been on the phone, and she could barely make anyone out. Tiny paws pitter-pattered by her feet, almost running past, and Charly reached down, scooping up Doll in her arms. She didn't know how such a tiny thing had gotten down the bus stairs. "Where's Sully?" she finally asked Eight. Since they'd known each other, Sully always seemed to be right there, so his not being around was strange. She could see Eight's head move in the darkness, or could she?

"On the bus. He's kind of busy."

Charly laughed. "Busy? Yeah, right. He can't be doing anything except sleeping or going to the bathroom, and I may be wrong, but I think the lavatories only work with power."

"I dunno," Eight said, then turned his back on her. "But I'm headed back to the bus. I think Driver's fixing it. You coming?"

Charly crinkled her brows together. Eight was a strange one, but Sully had said that he'd come on the road trip for him and to chaperone. Maybe he was Sully's personal as-sistant or something, she guessed. With Doll in her hands, she ran past Eight and climbed the bus's stairs. In the dark, she felt her way toward the bunk area and found her bag hanging on a hook. She grabbed it, then un-plugged her phone from the socket and stuck it inside her purse. The leash was sticking out the side of the bag. "Marlow. Marlow?" she called in a loud whisper, then felt Marlow at her feet. She didn't know why she felt the need to be quiet, but it was something about being in the dark that made her feel it necessary.

Bending down, she felt for Marlow's collar, then hooked the leash onto it with one hand. A deep moan pulled her attention, and she recognized Sully's voice. He sounded as if he was in major pain.

"You need help?" Eight asked, suddenly back on the bus. He walked over by Charly, making his way through the tiny space between her and the bunk. Sully groaned again. "I see you have both dogs. You need me to hold one or something?" Eight asked, turning up his voice as if he wanted to drown out Sully's groans.

"No, I'm fine. I was thinking about taking them out, but I think I'm gonna lay it down for a second," Charly said, craning her neck to try to make out Sully in the darkness. He moaned again. "Is he okay?" Charly asked, gripping Marlow's collar and balancing Doll at the same time. "On second thought, I think I can use some help. I'll nap later."

"Yes. Sully's all right. Always is," Eight said, making his way to the kitchen area and totally ignoring Charly. From where she stood, she could see Eight open the refrigerator, take out something large and set it on the counter. Marlow started to cry. "I'll wake you up when we get to Chicago or when help comes," he said to her. "You just go ahead and get some rest."

"Okay," Charly said to him, nodding. She eased her way to the front of the bus without him knowing. She didn't know what was up with Sully, and she could tell that Eight didn't want her to, which was fine. She was more interested in getting Marlow outside to relieve herself than worrying about who knew what. On her way down the stairs, she smiled when she heard the engine cough and the camera crew clap, but she kept her words and excitement to herself as she slipped undetected behind the crowd standing a few feet in front of the bus. She was tired, and wasn't up to idle chatter or a million watts of camera lights in her face, filming her. All Charly really needed was a few minutes alone—hundreds of seconds with just her and the dogs, she told herself. Then things would be better and she'd be her old self.

"Go Driver!" someone cheered.

"I do what I can, but nothing's promised. Yet," Driver bragged, flicking a lighter to partially illuminate a DIY engine guide.

Charly rounded the back of the bus and met pure darkness. For a second she stood, staring off into the nothingness, waiting for her eyes to adjust. Marlow scampered at her feet, pulling on the leash. "Okay, okay, Marlow," Charly said, walking Marlow down the dark road, careful to stay on the side of the street. Holding Doll in one arm and letting Marlow pull her other, she looked to the sky that went on forever and felt as if she were walking on it. It was that clear, that beautiful. It stretched before her like a sparkling magic carpet, and before Charly knew it, she was searching for Ursa Minor.

"There," she said, pointing to the heavens, trying to focus on what looked like a connect-the-dot dipper. "I see it, Marlow. I think . . ."

A crunching, rattling sound snatched her attention and made Marlow bark and dance. Behind her, the bus's engine roared to life. Charly turned, ready to yell out at the red brake lights that now glowed, but froze. There, on the ground in front of her and Marlow, something made a noise and moved. Slithered? Crouched? *Oh. God.* Charly didn't know what to do. Ever so slowly, she tightened Marlow's leash around her hand and reeled Marlow in closer, millimeter by millimeter, afraid that whatever it was would harm them if they moved too suddenly. Marlow whined, wanting to get to whatever it was in front of them. Doll growled. Charly tilted her head. Something had just hissed, she thought. Then the bus yawned and squeaked, the motor hummed and then shushed as if telling her to be quiet. But Charly knew better. The bus wasn't warning her of anything. The *shh* sound was a forewarning of what she heard next. The tour bus pulled off, and Charly watched it go. There was no way she could catch up to her ride. There was also no way she could scream without whatever-it-was attacking her and Marlow and Doll, and she was pretty sure that whatever-it-was was a snake. It had to be, she believed, staring as if glaring would summon the light to reveal to her what was on the ground.

A semi truck blew past, pushing a dirty breeze her way and offering a hint of light from its beams. And Charly saw it. A black snake was on the ground just a few feet in front of her and Marlow. Without thinking, she forgot about keeping still, and tightened her hold on Doll as she scooped up Marlow. Her feet connected with her butt as she ran like an Olympian down the middle of the road, too scared to realize that she was moving opposite the way the tour bus had gone, until it was too late and she was too tired to keep running.

* * *

She'd been walking and watching the stars forever. At least that's what it felt like. It was cold, dark, and creepy, but she couldn't let the scary trio deter her. The bus hadn't come back for her and the dogs, and she knew it probably wouldn't. Not until it was too late. She'd made Eight believe she was taking a nap, and was sure everyone probably thought she was tucked behind the curtain that separated her bunk from view. Charly kept pushing straight ahead. Darkness surrounded her on all sides, so it didn't matter which way she went. Up in the distance, a faint light pulled her attention. She didn't know if it was her imagination or not, but it seemed welcoming, like a hint of civilization. It also seemed to be moving farther away with each step, yet it appeared to get lighter every time her feet connected to the ground. Charly exhaled. She was sure she'd traveled a mile or more, but all would be okay, she believed. Especially when she spotted signage telling her that the light in the distance belonged to a truckers' gas station with a convenience store and diner.

"Yes!" she said, finally putting Marlow back on the ground. "In a second, Doll," she assured the tiny red pooch, knowing Doll probably had to go too, but Charly had only one leash, so the two of them had to share.

The cracked concrete of the gas station was under her feet before she knew it. Inhaling the truck fumes, she smiled, then squinted to adjust to the light. Charly was glad not to be drowned in almost complete darkness anymore. Her eyes surveyed the truck stop, and landed on a fleet of eighteen-wheelers parked in the distance. People moved around and drivers came and went, and Charly

took it all in. Yes, she'd reached civilization. She just didn't
know which.

"You lost?" a male voice asked.

Marlow barked and wagged her tail. Doll moved in
Charly's arms, trying to get down. Charly's heart did a
thu-thump behind her ribs, feeling like a hammer banging in her chest cavity. "It's you?" she asked, knowing who
it was without looking. His accent gave him away.

His laugh came out low and sexy, more like a moan.
"Liam," he said, offering his name as if she'd forgotten.
As if anyone could ever forget who he was, which Charly
doubted with everything inside her. Forgetting Liam was
akin to forgetting to breathe.

Charly turned. She felt her face stiffen, and knew she
wore a look of shock, though she didn't know why.
She'd known exactly whom she was going to see before
she'd turned. Liam had even told her. She'd turned to
stone because his masculine beauty was mesmerizing and
rendered her incapable of doing anything but stare, she
told herself. "Hi," she managed to say, and could've
kicked herself for sounding so stupid. There they were, in
the middle of nowhere, in the darkness of night, and all
she could come up with was *hi*?

Liam smiled. "Well, hello to you too, love," he
greeted, winking. "What are you doing here?" he began,
then looked around. "Wait a moment. Where's your tour
bus? Where's the crew?"

Charly shrugged, loving the way he'd called her *love*
and wondering if it was a name solely for her, or was it
his way of addressing girls—like the way some guys from
London called other guys blokes. She shook her head.

She was giving his use of the word *love* too much thought. "It's just me and Marlow and Doll. The others left," she began, then explained what had gone down.

Liam dug his hands in his jeans pockets, then kicked at loose gravel. He nodded. "I get it, love. I do." He began walking toward the expanse of openness that led to the diner, which was set out in the distance as if purposely trying to separate itself from the gas station. Charly and the dogs followed. Liam exhaled. "We stopped because I had to breathe for a moment. It's too crowded on the bus. Way too many people jammed inside. It feels sorta like a can of sardines."

Charly was sure Liam's complaint was valid, but his delectable accent made it all seem like it wasn't so bad. She paused. "Wait. I thought you took a jet everywhere."

Liam stopped, nodded, then laughed. He kicked at the gravel again. "Guess you heard I was too good to take a tour bus too. That I'm a bit, well . . . standoffish? Better than everyone else, I suppose? Boy Wonder, huh, love?" he asked, winking again.

Charly shrugged. "Well, I wouldn't say all of that, but, ya know?" She smiled, knowing her *ya know* gave it away. Yes, she'd heard Liam was better than everyone else, or believed he was.

Liam took Doll from Charly and leaned in toward her ear. "Well, looks like you may be the only one who gets to know me, Charly. I mean, since we're now touring together." He tilted his head in the direction his bus was parked. "It's a bonus for me, though, love. I want to know you. You're different, in a good way," he whispered, then set the dog on the ground.

8

There was no way she could get on the tour bus with him; the huge tour bus with the word JET written across it. She laughed. There had been some truth to Sully's saying Liam took a jet everywhere he went, just not in the literal flying-in-the-air sense. No, she couldn't ride with him. He was too gorgeous, and his raspy voice was heart melting. There was no way she could let him take her to Chicago. She was too afraid that somewhere on the highway between wherever they were and their destination, she'd fall for him. His looks were enough to make any living, breathing girl question having a relationship with anyone besides him. Even Mason.

"Charly," he said, standing two feet from her while Doll emptied her bladder, "you know I can't and won't leave you out here. Since we're going to be starring on the same series and now traveling together, we might as well get to know each other. Wouldn't you say?"

God, his accent rattled her. It stole every bit of cool she possessed and warmed her to the core. The drive to Chicago was going to be long. Too long, she told herself, thinking about Mason, who, despite it all, was her boyfriend, whether they were into it or not. She nodded. Yes, she wanted to know Liam. She wanted to know him like she wanted to be the best actress in the world. And keeping her distance and pretending to view him only as a costar would put her actress skills to the test. She'd be Oscar worthy by the time they finished taping the first show.

Liam held out his hand to her. "C'mon, love. We may as well get this over with. The cameras are waiting."

Charly took his hand and gulped. She'd had enough of cameras and cameramen already. In just the short time she'd been blinded by all the wattage, just moments before the bus broke down, she'd grown not to like them. She'd rather they be saved for the show's taping. "You have a crew on your bus, too?"

Liam nodded, stopping in front of the bus. "Yes, unfortunately. But my camera crew is here for two reasons. I'm, of course, doing our show, *The Extreme Dream Team*, but I'm also doing a video diary for the video channel here in the States. One will help play the other up—the *Dream Team* show and the *Behind the Scenes with Liam* diary." He winked. "I bet it'll help you too." He shrugged, then began to walk up the stairs, pulling her along. "If you want . . . I mean, there's plenty of room in the spotlight, and I don't mind sharing." He turned to her. "Now, tell me why you're here. How'd you get cast on the series?"

Charly stepped on the bus, smiling. She gritted her teeth and kept her lips wide, prepared for the camera crew. If she couldn't do anything else, she could be the star they expected her to be because she was born for the role. And that's exactly what she told Liam when she finished telling him of her epic adventures that had landed her on the series. When the cameras weren't rolling, she told him everything else, even the parts about the lies, her once missing father she pretended to fly to New York to visit, whom she now lived with, and how many times her mother had stolen from and mistreated her. Charly couldn't believe how easy it was, talking to Liam. He'd asked her a simple question, and she'd bombarded him with truth. And it felt good. She'd never been so honest before.

"You're brave," he told her, then kissed her lightly on the cheek. "Braver than most adult men. Question?"

"Answer," Charly replied, laughing.

"So since you're from Illinois, is there anything you suggest I see or do besides the usual tourist stuff when we're there? A restaurant I should eat at, perhaps?"

Charly laughed. "Do you like popcorn? There's this mom-and-pop place there that sells caramel and chocolate–covered popcorn that's sprinkled with pecans. It's different, and they're the only place that makes it, that I know of. It's my favorite . . ." she began, then settled in. The ride to Chicago was going to be eventful, she thought, finally breathing after getting used to the cameras and microphones being in her face. Liam, to her dismay, had lived up to his handsomeness and delectable accent. She'd silently hoped that he'd stumble over his words, say something stupid that would turn her off. But no, he'd done just the opposite. He'd intrigued her, then held her attention with his story. Like her, he'd always wanted to be on television, but was a bit different because he didn't consider himself an actor. He'd smiled at her, then told her how he'd moved from "across the pond" to attend some elite prep school that had scouted him because of his rowing ability, which impressed Charly. She didn't know that schools had rowing teams, and really hated to admit that she didn't know what one was. Who knew schools scouted people to row boats? Or that people got Ivy League university scholarships because of it? She laughed at herself. She'd been so in the dark before moving to the East Coast, and was grateful for finally getting the light she so needed, including the limelight she'd now be sharing with him. Yes, Liam was refreshing. He was a breath of fresh air and trouble waiting to happen. She could feel it. He'd snatched her admiration when he'd told her that he'd walked away from everything—the elite prep school, the rowing team, and more-than-a-possibility of attending an Ivy League college—to live his dream after Mr. Day had discovered him in a home renovation store.

"Yeah, I was there to buy wood to finish building a boat, and there Mr. Day was, staring and smiling. He asked two questions, then my world changed." Liam grinned, tossing her a look, then turned his attention back to a sketchbook he was doodling bedroom designs in. He was preparing plans for the furniture he was going to make for the little girl they were going to surprise with a bedroom/office makeover.

"What did he ask?" Charly was curious.

"He asked if I was handy at carpentry, which I am. I can design and build just about anything. Then he asked if I wanted to be a star, and of course I said yes." He threw her a quick wink, then turned the drawing pad around so she could see it. "What d'you think? You think the girl will like it?"

Charly nodded at his design, thinking it was as wonderful as their entire conversation had been, and how wonderful talking to him had made her feel. It was nice to know someone who'd wanted something as badly as she, and even better to know he'd be on the road with the show. "It's perfect. Really perfect, Liam. I see why you're in such demand."

"And in the morning, I'll get to see why you're in such top demand, Charly," he teased, winking.

"Tomorrow morning? I thought we were jumping right into the taping."

He shook his head no, then nodded yes. "Yes. In a few hours we have to do a run-through. That way you and the local crew—there's one local crew for every show—get a feel for the taping. I believe it's more for you and me. This is my first time doing a reality series here in the States, and I think they want to pretend to break you in on how it goes, while at the same time breaking me in. You don't mind, do you, love?"

Charly nodded, then shook her head. Being so close to Liam was causing confusion between what her mind said—*be professional*—and what her heart was urging—*he's fine and you're on the road with him*. Charly smiled, sure her skin was tinted crimson. With Mason, she'd been uneasy too, but in a different way. Mason made her nervous and want to be everything she thought he thought she was. All the thinking about what *she* thought *he* thought was confusing. With Liam she felt something different, something more kindred. Probably because of the series, she told herself. Yes, that had to be it. She was naturally drawn to Liam because they had something in common besides big cities and small towns, the things that had brought her and Mason together. "It's cool." She yawned, then stretched.

Liam laughed. "Well"—he paused, looking at her outstretched arms and long legs—"I might mind. If you're going to be looking so beautiful all the time, you may distract me." He laughed again. "You can sleep in my bunk, if you like. I'll crash here. We've only a few hours left before we arrive, so get some sleep."

Charly nodded. She was tired and wouldn't fight him on sleeping—especially not on his bunk. She loved that he was gentlemanly enough to give her his bed, almost as much as she loved his accent. No matter how often she heard it, Charly knew she'd never get used to it. It was so scrumptious to her ears, she couldn't hear it enough. She inhaled, then tried to breathe easy as she made her way to where he rested his head. They'd soon be in Chicago, and she had to be ready.

LIFE OF A
TELEVISION STAR

9

———

Charly's eyes bulged and lit up while watching Chicago transform from the Windy City to the city of the fabulous; at least that's how she felt seeing the room change. A desk moved in front of her like it had human legs instead of four inanimate ones, and seemed to be scampering to and fro, until just the right location was found, which was dictated by Liam's, "Yes, right there. Perfect!"

"Whaddya think?" Annison asked Charly while overhead cameras and lights were pointed at them.

Charly nodded and grinned at Marlow, who was just off the set with a handler. Her dog was behind the cameras and crew, but still within Charly's sight, which she'd demanded. Mr. Day had told her that there was no way the studio would go for pets on the set because that would change the entire concept of the show, but had agreed for Marlow to tour with her. Annison had Doll, so there was really no way he could argue against Marlow's tagging along. "I think it's great, and I know that Elisa will too," Charly began, then reminded the audience about the recipient's achievements and why Elisa was chosen by *The Extreme Dream Team* for a makeover. "After being the class president and valedictorian at her school, and founding RMAH, which stands for Raising Money and Awareness for the Homeless, Elisa deserves this makeover."

Annison nodded, smiling like a supermodel, and just as fake as one too. For some reason, many of her grins seemed superficial, and there was a certain blankness behind her eyes that made her seem lifeless. Charly wondered what had made Annison seem so unhappy, but whatever it was was becoming more apparent. "I agree, Charly. She certainly does."

"Absolutely, she does!" Liam's voice came from behind, followed by his hands, which tickled Charly. "I just thought I'd pop over and see if you two girls need anything before I head back outside."

Charly giggled, swatting Liam away. "We're great in here. Thanks." Her voice trailed off and her hands reached toward her pants. "Speaking of she," Charly began, then took her phone out of her pocket. "That's Elisa calling now." Charly began to walk away from the furniture movers and noise, then looked at Annison for the sign to answer Elisa's call.

Annison knocked on the window, held her finger to her mouth to quiet the noise outside the house, then shushed the crew inside. Finally she held up her thumb in the air, signaling it was okay to take the call.

Charly smiled into the camera as she spoke to Elisa, making sure she was expressive and very friendly. She nodded as she spoke, then ended the call. "She's about ten minutes away! Let's go meet her."

"You two go ahead," Annison said to Charly and Liam. "I just need to make sure all is perfect here. I don't want a thing out of place for Elisa. She deserves the best. Besides"—she nodded and moved her head toward the outside—"it's too dirty out there for me. You know I like to keep it clean." Her smile was huge, and so was Liam's display of rolling his eyes in the most masculine way a guy could.

Liam held out his arm to Charly. "Your guide awaits, Madame Charly," he said, winking and smiling.

Charly stuck her arm though Liam's. "Well, thank you, good sir. I couldn't ask for a better one. Off to Lady Elisa, please." She flirted and joked, changing her American English accent into his Queen's English accent and playing it up for the cameras because she was having fun.

Liam nudged her when their backs were to the cameras, then showed her his palm. In black marker was written: Party 2nite @ the dox. Yes?

Charly nodded and smiled, but this time her grin was reserved strictly for him.

Charly's cell screen informed her that she'd received twelve calls since the taping had begun. She shook her head and laughed. Her best friend, Lola, was staying true to her character, calling back-to-back despite knowing Charly wouldn't be able to answer. Charly rotated her head, trying to work out some of the kinks. She'd been a bit anxious about the first show, and that had made her tense. "Thank you," she said, taking first Marlow and then her messenger bag from an assistant. She shouldered the bag, deciding to call Lola once she got back to the bus. She gripped Marlow's leash, then popped some cheesy fries into her mouth, which she'd swiped from the spread of food the caterers had set up in a tent. "Come on, Marlow. Let's go get some rest."

"Good show, Charly," someone complimented her as she walked toward the bus, parked down the block and out of sight from Elisa's home to ensure it'd be out of the way of the cameras.

"Fabulous job, Charly. You're a natural," another said.

"The newest reality star," came one more compliment.

"Thank you, guys. You're all the best. Really. You made it so easy for me," she said, walking backward so she could face them while she expressed her gratitude, then turned toward the bus with Marlow following. She couldn't wait to shower and nap. The day had been long, and she needed to be rested for the party. She stuck more fries into her mouth and licked the cheese off her lips.

"Hey, superstar! Where ya going?" Annison yelled out, stopping Charly as she passed Annison's bus.

Charly smiled. Annison calling her a star was the biggest compliment she could've received. "Thanks, but really . . . we both know who the star of the show is."

Annison waved away Charly's flattery. "Where are you going?"

Charly shrugged, suddenly not sure *to my bus* was the

right answer, but that's where she was headed. "To take a nap . . . ?"

Annison beckoned her. "Well, you might as well ride with me. Come hop on my bus. We're not leaving until the morning, so we're in hotels tonight. You didn't get the updated itinerary yet, I'm assuming. We can do what we want tonight—i.e., go to the party—but we've got an early morning."

"Early? Why early? We're not leaving yet, are we?" Charly inquired, sticking a few more fries into her mouth.

Annison nodded, then shook her head as she looked at Charly's choice of food with a hint of disgust. "Yes, we're *flying* to Atlanta."

Charly reared back her head. "Flight? To Atlanta? So soon?"

Annison laughed. "Eventually, but no Atlanta just yet. It only seems as if we're taping back-to-back. I just figured we should hit the town early and do some morning shopping . . . before the stores are packed and I get mobbed." She shrugged. "After you disappeared and your bus broke down . . ." She shook her head. "Trust me, none of us wanted to bus it across country, anyway. It was only for camera coverage, I'm sure." Annison pushed her hair out of her face with a book in hand, batted her long lashes, then dug into a bag and pulled out an apple. The book had disappeared, and Charly assumed it was either on the table or in the bag. "Hurry up. There has to be a Jacuzzi waiting for me somewhere." She turned and looked over her shoulder. "Hello!" she called out to someone Charly couldn't see and assumed was one of Annison's assistants. When there was no response, she said, "Can you believe no one is here to wash or cut this apple for me? Something's going on with the water supply on this bus. Charly, can you be a doll and rinse this off before we leave?" She thrust the apple out of the window.

Charly smiled. Annison wasn't like anyone she knew. She possessed that air of confidence that probably came from her practically being born a star, and oozed it when she talked. She seemed cool but was still different. Charly couldn't imagine her going to a regular school or looking forward to getting a driver's license. She couldn't see her having a worry in the world besides needing someone to cut her fruit. "What book was that?" she had to ask.

"Book? What book? Oh you mean the magazine?" Annison lied. She had been holding a book. "Come on, Charly," she said, ignoring the question and avoiding giving an answer. "If you hang on the set, people will start to treat you like you hang on the set . . . and eat fast food. Follow my example. I normally play my part then depart—that's what I do. But since this show is based on reality, I do what I'm supposed to do, then I leave because sometimes I just don't feel like acting or being on camera or whatever." She shrugged. "So, about my apple?"

Charly shook her head, unable to relate to Annison not always feeling up to acting. She shrugged too, then nodded. She appreciated Annison's advice, but she wasn't Annison. "Thanks, Annison. I appreciate you sharing. But I'd rather do this my way. My way works for me." She shrugged, then stuck a few fries into her mouth.

"Sorry. I don't do other people's fruit, but I *do* do fast food." She threw her costar a nasty look, then walked off. "Marlow's gotta pee."

"Come on, Charly. It's not that big a deal," Annison said. "I'm only trying to save your figure and career."

Charly rolled her eyes. No, Annison wasn't like anyone she knew, and she guessed Annison didn't know anyone like Charly, either.

Lola was waiting for her in the sitting area of the hotel lobby, with her legs crossed, popping gum. In her hand was a folded magazine, and on her face was an it's-about-time scowl. Charly's eyes saucered at the sight of her friend.

"Do you know how long I've been here, Charly?" Lola asked, standing and tossing the magazine on a coffee table. She ran her hand over her naturally blond porcupine-ish styled hairdo and slowly batted her ocean-blue eyes. "Huh?" she asked, snaking her neck and wiping pretend sweat from her cinnamon skin.

Charly just rolled her eyes and smiled. "I don't even know how you knew where I was staying. I just found out myself." She held out her arms. "You know you want to hug me . . . all that calling. You missed your best friend, right?" she asked.

Lola popped her gum, then sucked her teeth. "Whatever, Charly St. James. Why didn't you call me back? Do you realize how much traveling I had to do to get here? It's not like the Chi is minutes away from my crib. I had to bus it, bus it again, train it, then cab it to get here," she complained, finally giving in, walking over and giving

Charly a one-armed hug until the count of three, a time frame they'd come up with that seemed appropriate for a sisterly hug.

"There's a party," Charly said, dangling the bait. "Why didn't you bring Stormy?"

Lola rolled her eyes. "She wasn't answering her phone or the door. She'd mentioned people coming by the house, then she said something about being scouted for some extreme science fair a couple of towns over. That's where she went, I'm sure," Lola said, then smiled, pursing her lips. She stepped back and picked up Marlow, cradling her like a baby. "Party, huh? Really? Whose?"

Charly shrugged. "We're here for television, so it's probably some industry party, I guess."

"Hmm," Lola said, holding one finger in front of her lips as if she was thinking about it. "I guess I could," she began. She bent over, then stood again. It took only two steps before Charly noticed Lola had brought an overnight bag with her. "A girl has to be prepared, ya know?"

Charly nodded, laughing. "Yes. I see."

Lola shook her head. "Oh, I wasn't talking about me, Charly. You know I'm always on top of it. I was talking about you."

Charly's eyebrows crinkled.

Lola grinned like a Cheshire cat. "You know Mason's here, right?"

Charly's jaw almost hit the floor.

"Well, let's go," Lola said, and walked away carrying Marlow in one arm and wheeling an overnight bag with the other. "Let's get to our room. I'm tired after all that traveling. You know my house is like seventy miles from here?" she rattled on, making her way to the bank of elevators.

A loud group of people walked by Charly, and she snapped out of her daze. Hoisting up her messenger bag on her shoulder, she walked quickly to the elevators, catching up with Lola.

"So when you say Mason's here, do you mean *here* like in the city of Chicago, or *here* like he's back in the state of Illinois?"

Lola's eyes bulged and she did a double take, looking at something over Charly's shoulder. "Oh, sweet Jesus," she said, and made Charly laugh.

"You sound like you're eighty or something, Lola. And you're such a sinner, so this has to be good," Charly said, then looked over her shoulder and saw Sully. She turned and faced Lola. "I know, he's different with all the tattoos and the grimace, but he's—"

"He's gorgeous, and the tattoos look good on him. Is his face pierced?" she asked, nodding. "Interesting."

"He's also a bit, well . . . mean."

Lola tapped her foot. "So who is he?"

"That's just Sully. He's on the show. Now, back to Mason."

"Uh-uh," Lola said, shaking her head in the negative. "Introduce me, Charly. Please? You have to. Heck, I'm not exactly nice. I can tame him. Hook me up," she urged, walking around Charly and tugging on Charly's messenger-bag strap.

There was no use, Charly thought. There was no way Lola was going to change her mind or give up information on Mason if Charly didn't cooperate and introduce her best friend to her costar. "Okay, okay," Charly said, giving in. "Let's hurry up though. I need to shower."

"Okay," Lola agreed, pasting a sneerlike smile on her face and eyeing Sully. "I agree. Especially since Mason will be here in less than an hour. You're meeting downtown . . . sorta."

10

The wind blew in Charly's face as she made her way down Michigan Avenue, the sorta downtown area Lola was talking about, which wasn't really downtown at all. To her left was a drugstore; to her right, across the street by the bookstore, a large group of people sang while they walked. Charly smiled, enjoying the vibe of Chicago's Gold Coast, which was where the upper crust of the city lived. She looked down at her phone. Mason's text had asked her to meet him at the Water Tower, and though she wasn't too familiar with the area, her phone's GPS told her she was less than a block away. And she knew of the Water Tower Place shopping complex from her mother. Anytime her mom would shop somewhere other than their small town or a local mall, it was big news.

Charly's heart skipped as she approached the tall structure, then fluttered when her hand pulled open the heavy door trimmed in gold and she stepped inside the building, greeted by the sight of escalators in front of her. She was only a couple minutes away from seeing her boyfriend, and she was nervous. And it wasn't a good feeling either. Mason had been a pain in her butt for all the wrong reasons, and she didn't understand why, but somehow she felt it was all her fault. But she hadn't done anything, she reminded herself. There was no way she was going to let Mason make her feel guilty for his insecurities and his jumping to conclusions, which is exactly what he'd done. He'd hopped from one wrong idea to another, until he'd pieced together a lopsided puzzle with pieces that didn't match.

"Excuse me," Charly said to a couple who were blocking her way, then stepped on the escalator. She was going to meet him on the second floor.

A hand was on her shoulders, squeezing her collarbone from behind. Without turning around, Charly knew it was Mason. "Aren't you the star from TV?" he asked jokingly, sounding like the younger girls Charly had met in the airport when she'd gone to pick up Mason in New York. "I saw your commercial," he said, his tone now different. "It was nice. Very nice, Charly. You're good for the camera. Really."

Charly turned and smiled. Mason's compliments meant a lot to her, and so did his expression. His ultracute face had the same welcoming expression she'd remembered, and it made her feel good. There wasn't a scowl or unspoken accusation on it. His lips spread until his grin matched hers. "Thank you, Mason. I'm glad to see you're back to your old self."

Mason grabbed her hand, pulling her down the ascending stairs. "Come on," he said to her, then apologized to the people who were behind them as they walked by and Mason's shopping bag bumped them.

Charly laughed. It was just like Mason to do something so backward and make it seem so right, she thought, going down the wrong way. With him, whatever was meant to go down he made go up, and vice versa. That was one of the things she'd always loved about him. He didn't fit into the world; he made the world fit him. Just like she did.

"I was just thinking we should've met near the chocolate-popcorn spot you love so much. It's just a train ride or two away from here, I think," he said.

Charly beamed. Sure, she wanted her popcorn. Who didn't and who wouldn't? "Chocolate and caramel with pecans?" She poked out her lips as if pouting, then puppy-dogged her eyes.

Mason shook his head, tightening his grip on her hand and pulling her outside onto the street. He laughed out loud. "This way. And, Charly? Stop the dramatics and save it for the cameras!" He glanced at her. "Yes, you can have your chocolate and caramel popcorn."

"With pecans, not walnuts? The biggest size they sell?" she asked, her pout still on her face.

Mason reared back his head and pressed his lips together in thought. He shrugged. "I thought we could

shoot over there *after* I go buy this hat I saw. But . . . ?"
he trailed off.

"But what?" Charly asked, excited and a bit confused.
She didn't understand his hesitation. He knew she'd want
her favorite treat; she always did. "But what, Mason?"

He smiled, then held up the shopping bag he held.
"But I decided to get it first and bring it to you. Kinda
like a I'm-sorry-for-being-a-pain gift."

Charly let go of his hand, then wrapped him in a hug.
"Thank you, Mason. That's so sweet." She finally released him, then took the shopping bag and began digging in it.

"Wait." He drew his brows together. "Don't thank me
yet. I didn't get the biggest size." He shrugged again. "I
couldn't afford the biggest and the hat. Sorry."

The night was moving fast. Too quickly, Charly thought,
walking down the street holding on to Mason's hand as if
she were a toddler and he her protector. They'd been having such a good time that she was afraid to let him go. It
seemed like forever since they'd been so close, just hanging out and talking about nothing and everything.

Mason stopped on the corner, pulling her back so she
wouldn't walk into the street. "So, what now?" he asked,
gripping the shopping bag that housed her popcorn.

Charly smiled, straightened his new hat, and shrugged.
"Well, there's this party going on tonight. It's supposed
to be a big deal, I think. And I'm expected to go because
it's for the cast of the show."

Mason nodded. "That's cool. I didn't expect to get all

of your time. I'm just glad to be able to hang out with a celebrity." He forced a smile.

Charly punched him in the arm. "You're coming with, right?"

He made a big deal of rubbing where she'd punched. "You're stronger than I thought," he said. "So you want me to go?"

Now Charly rolled her eyes. "Of course. Why would I bring up the party if I didn't want you to go?"

He shrugged. "Maybe because I couldn't afford the biggest popcorn," he joked, but Charly could tell that he was disappointed because he'd said something about it twice. He mentioned it as soon as they'd left the hat store and now.

"Whatever. So is that a yes or no?" She held up her hand, trying to beckon a cab. "I need to run by the hotel, change, and check on Marlow. Oh, and get Lola . . . which means I should get Marlow too. I think everyone will be at the party, so there will be no sitter for her."

Mason playfully rolled his eyes. "I don't know about Marlow. But Lola would be a good idea. She has my clothes in her bag. She was convinced we were staying in the city, especially after I told her my older cousin lives on the West side and will let me crash at his spot. So she insisted—this was after she hunted me down and told me you'd be in town. She even sprung for the trip here . . . and you know she's cheap. But that's your girl. Your ride-till-y'all-die true one. You should know . . . she's your best friend."

"That she is," Charly said, thinking of how much Lola

had looked out for her. A cab pulled up in front of them, and she reached out and opened the door. "Let's go, Mason. We gotta get dressed and show the crew how partying is done!"

The water would've been too black to see if it hadn't shimmered like billows of silk under the moonlight. White ball lights were strung on poles that surrounded the patio and pool, outlining the yard, which stretched to the shore. Music blasted from a stage constructed five feet high, which had as many speakers as it had local band members.

Charly nodded, petting Marlow, who she'd insisted come along. She wasn't comfortable leaving Marlow in the hotel holed up in a carrier. "This is cool, right?" she said to Mason, who stood between her and Lola. Lola was gazing across the yard.

Mason agreed. "Yeah. This is actually real cool. I don't usually go for live bands, not unless it's like The Roots or somebody big, but this band is pretty tight."

Bobbing her head to the music, Charly realized Lola's body was there, but her mind was clearly somewhere else. "Lola? Lola?" She reached her hand across Mason's chest, then snapped her fingers in Lola's face to get her attention. "Lola?"

"What?" Lola asked, fixing her small red dress that clung to her curves.

Charly and Mason laughed.

"Good show, Charly," someone called out.

"Thanks," she called back.

"What?" Lola asked again. "Did you want something?"

Mason really laughed, then adjusted his jeans, which he wore with a button-down shirt, a fresh pair of sneakers, and the new hat he'd bought. "No, we don't want anything, but obviously you do," he teased.

"Just go see him, Lola. Talk to him," Charly said, nodding her head toward where Sully stood, then rearing back her head when she saw he was checking out Lola as much as Lola was digging on him. "I know I probably made him sound awful and rude, but Sully's cool. He's real."

"You won't be mad? I mean, I did come here to hang with you. We haven't seen each other in—"

"There's nothing I can do for you that he can," Charly said, cutting her off. "Besides, you gave me my present, and I couldn't thank you enough." She winked at Mason.

"Well, here, let me take her," Lola said, taking Marlow from Charly and setting her on the ground. "Dogs always serve as good conversation excuses with guys, for some reason. Animals and sports."

"Nah. Not this time, Lola," Charly warned.

"No?" Lola asked, shaking her head. "You mean I can just be myself?"

Charly nodded. "Yep. Only yourself. He hates phony people, according to him."

Lola nodded. "Cool. I hate pretending anyway. If I don't have to talk sports, he's my kinda dude." She walked away with Marlow pitter-pattering next to her.

Mason grabbed Charly's hand and laced his fingers through hers. "Ready? You said you have to be here, so I guess that means we should make the rounds before we disappear by the water. I think it'd be nice to go for a walk."

She crinkled her nose. She loved when Mason flirted, and was happy to witness it face-to-face. Their relationship had been built over the phone after she'd left Illinois and moved to New York, so they'd never really spent quality time with each other. The moments they'd spent together before the relocation were equivalent to them both fronting. She'd pretended she didn't like him and he'd pretended not to know. She was just about to tell him that she was ready, that she'd love nothing more than to disappear with him, when she realized she couldn't.

"Ah, Charly . . . Charly, Charly, Charly," Mr. Day said, making his way across the lawn.

Charly smiled, then Mason let go of her hand, making her grin fade. "Hi, Mr. Day. What are you doing here?" she asked.

He thrust his forehead in her direction as if he were playing soccer and bouncing a ball off his head. "You. Seems you disappeared, and as you know, the people on your bus had a meltdown—rightfully so, and the troops were called in." He pointed to his chest. "I'm the troops."

Charly gulped, trying to keep her heart down in her chest where it belonged. She was sure it was going to come out of her throat from nervousness and guilt. She hadn't really done anything wrong, but for some reason she thought Mr. Day would think so. "Well . . . I . . . They left me, Mr. Day," she said, defending herself.

Mr. Day laughed, waving away her explanation. "Don't

worry about it, Charly. I had to fly in anyway. It's a normal thing for me; I attend all the first press junkets." He
turned toward Mason. "Do you mind if I borrow her
for a moment? We've got a bout of interviews to do.
Well, I have one, she has many. Then she's all yours.
Promise."

Mason smiled, took off his new hat, rubbed his hand
over his hair, then put it back on, adjusting it to face
front. "Of course."

"Also, we're doing the interviews differently with this
show. I've teamed up Annison and Sully, and you and
Liam. I think it's better not to have the partners together;
that way one doesn't outshine or upstage the other. See
you in there." Mr. Day walked away.

"I'll be back as soon as the interviews are over," she
said, watching Mr. Day disappear into a huge tent that
she hadn't noticed before. She'd been so consumed with
Mason, she hadn't really taken a good look around.

He nodded. "I'll go find Lola. If you have to do the interviews, that means ol' boy that she's with has to do
them too. Right?"

"Yes, that'd be Sully," Charly said, nodding. "I wonder if we'll be interviewed in separate rooms, or rather on
separate sides of the tent."

"You're beautiful, Charly. You know that?" Mason
said.

She leaned in to give him a kiss as a thank-you.

"Hey, Charly," a voice called out, stopping her mid-
smooch.

She grimaced and melted all at the same time. Liam's
voice was making her knees turn to mush, but she hated

that he'd interrupted her kissing Mason. The sound of his footsteps quickly making his way toward them made her turn around.

"Here," Liam said, handing her a big, bulging bag. "I know you're probably a little nervous about your first set of interviews, so I thought this would make you feel better."

Charly took the bag, weighing it in her hands. "What's this?"

Liam smiled. "Remember you told me about the popcorn you liked so much here? Well, I pulled some strings and found out where to get it. It wasn't easy, but it seems with just the description, someone knew. You never told me the name of the place, and even if you had, I probably wouldn't have found it. The place doesn't even have a legible sign," he rattled on. "Anyway, I went to get you the biggest size they sell. Chocolate and caramel and nuts or something or other, or is it butter?" He shook his head at his own question. "Nah, it wouldn't be butter—you're not a butter type of girl. Too plain, right?" he asked Mason.

"Yo, dude. You better watch yourself. You're being real disrespectful, and I know what you're up to. Whaddya mean, she's not the butter type—too plain? Whaddya trying to say?" Mason stepped up. "You already played it too close back in New York. Don't act up here. Just like New York, Illinois is my playground too."

Liam stood his ground. He didn't say a word, but he didn't move either.

Charly stood in front of Mason. "I don't think he means

anything, Mason. He's just trying to be nice. Right, Liam?" Charly asked, then bit her tongue to prevent herself from smiling. Her pulse sped, thinking of how Mason must've felt. He couldn't afford to buy her the large size. But she couldn't help but be impressed by Liam and all he'd gone through to find her popcorn. "You didn't have to do that. Seriously, you didn't have to get me any, and really the large is too much," she said for Mason's benefit. The truth was, a big-sized popcorn was exactly what she needed, and she'd stay up all night snacking on it.

Liam laughed, then playfully reached to pat Mason on the arm. Mason drew back and balled his fists at his sides. "It's no big deal, right? It's just popcorn. Who can't buy popcorn?" he asked, looking from Charly to Mason, shrugging his shoulders. He turned back to Charly. "And I didn't buy you one."

She exhaled. Maybe the studio had purchased it—that would be better for Mason's ego, she believed. Besides, Liam had said he'd *gotten* her popcorn, not *bought* it, she reasoned. "Well, so the studio paid for it? That's cool."

Liam shook his head. "Of course not, Charly. They give us caterers, not fund our whims. And the reason I didn't buy you one is because I bought you *two*. A huge one of the chocolate and caramel and nuts and another huge one with butter, just to be sure. I even brought you an empty bag so you could mix them together, but I think I left that in my room. I'll give it to you later." He threw Mason a look.

Mason lunged.

Charly stopped Mason, then looked at him. His breathing was labored and his temples were throbbing. His cloak of anger wasn't cloaked at all, it was see-through.

"Hurry, Charly and Liam. Annison and Sully just finished," Mr. Day was yelling. "It's your turn."

11

The cameras were flashing and Charly was smiling. She'd never done what Mr. Day had called a press junket, but she'd seen one or two played out on television and at the movies, and it was nothing like the real thing, she thought. Nor was it as huge as she'd imagined. She'd pictured an audience full of reporters with raised hands and microphones and just as many cameras as there were people. Her imagination had told her that a junket was like a scene at the White House when the president makes an announcement, or like the media circus right before a professional boxing match, when the boxers weigh in and toss threats at each other. Her idea was all wrong. Charly shook her head, then glanced down at her hand, which Liam was barely touching.

"So we heard you ran away, Charly?" a reporter asked.

Charly was just about to answer yes, when she felt Liam's leg bumping against hers. He quickly put a fist in front of his mouth, then cleared his throat. She took his leg bumping and sudden cough as signs not to answer. "Excuse me?" she asked the reporter, avoiding the question and buying time.

The lady reporter smiled. "Well, I received word that on your way here to Chicago, you ran away from your tour bus just so you could ride with Liam on his bus. Is that true?"

Liam's cough turned into a laugh, and he shook his head no. "Well, actually Charly didn't run away. I did. I did that *Star Trek* thing and had myself beamed onto her bus by Scotty. I believe that's what you guys call him. Scotty, right? It was all quite American," he finished, making everyone laugh. "Seems you really can get anything you want in this country. I'm glad I came over here to work." The audience of reporters laughed even louder, and so did Charly. "Otherwise I wouldn't have met Charly here, and discovered she loved this popcorn so much." He reached down, then held up one of the large bags of popcorn he'd given her, opened it, and tossed a few kernels into his mouth. "Oh my!" he exclaimed, widening his eyes at Charly and nodding. Again, the reporters laughed, most approvingly and knowingly, and a couple of them yelled out that they loved that popcorn too.

"I told you it's delicious," Charly said, then nudged her leg against Liam's as a way of thanking him for saving her. She wondered how the press had found out so quickly about her riding with him, then shrugged her shoulders. It really wasn't a big deal, at least no more of a big deal than her having a bus driver who didn't know where he was going—but she'd never tell that. Snitching just wasn't in her.

"And so are you, love. So are you." Liam flirted, winking and playing it up for the cameras.

Mr. Day, standing in the back of the tent, waved his arm high in the air to get her attention, then held up his index finger. Charly nodded, getting the message, then leaned forward. "One more question only, please? The cast and I would really like to get out and eat something, and I need to get back to my dog, Marlow."

Suddenly a dozen questions were tossed at her about Marlow, and Charly answered them all truthfully, including how she'd rescued Marlow, taken care of the tiny puppy when Charly was broke and moving from state to state, and why Marlow traveled with her now.

"So, pretty much, Marlow is like your baby?" another reporter asked.

Charly nodded, then her lips spread into a warm and welcoming smile. She outstretched her arms to receive Marlow as Mr. Day carried her dog down the aisle. "This is my baby, Marlow," she said. The cameras flashed nonstop for almost a minute before Liam stood, then carefully pulled out Charly's chair so she could do the same. He wrapped his arm around her, posing for a few more pictures, then it was over.

"Thanks for the save, Liam. I'll see you outside at the real party," Charly said before making her way toward the tent's exit. She had to go find Mason.

Marlow was in her arms as she made her way through the tent as quickly as she could. Reporters and other interviewers stopped her every few steps to say a quick hello or to try to sneak another question. Charly tried to be as cordial as she could, but she really had to go. Mason hadn't been too happy before she left, and she understood why. She wouldn't have felt too good either if she were in his position and some television personality one-upped her with a gift. Finally Lola appeared, pushing through the throngs of people.

"Charly, I've been waiting for you," she said, walking quickly toward Charly and positioning herself in front of someone waiting for Charly's attention. "What's the holdup?" Lola asked, sidestepping the person.

Charly drew her brows together. "Well, I was just on my way out. And you couldn't have been waiting too long. Mr. Day just gave me Marlow a few minutes ago, and he had to get her from you, right? You're the one I left her with."

"Sorry, I'll bring her right back. At least I'll try," Lola said to the person who was waiting on Charly, then grabbed Charly's free hand, pulling her toward the tent exit. "No, that's the thing, Charly. After Sully's interviews, he wanted to go for a walk, so I gave Marlow to Mason. He was in here watching your interviews, and that's how Mr. Day got Marlow."

Charly smiled. She didn't think Mason would be into watching her interview, and she thought it was sweet that he'd become so interested and was supporting her. He'd always seemed too smooth and cool for that. "Wow . . ."

Lola pulled her outside. She came toe-to-toe with Charly, her face more serious than Charly had seen it since Lola had discovered she was a love child. "No wow. Where."

Charly set Marlow on the ground. Instinctively she looked around, somehow sure that Mason wouldn't be easy to find. "What do you mean, *where*, Lola?"

Lola shrugged her shoulders, then nodded her head to the left as if to indicate a direction.

"Nope! That won't do, Lola. Just spill. If you know where Mason is . . . If you know something I don't, get to talking."

Lola rolled her eyes and pivoted. She began walking across the yard. "If you don't like what we find . . ."

"I can handle it. Don't you worry about it. You know me," Charly said. Her words were more of a warning for whoever was doing her wrong, if anyone was. She followed Lola across the lawn, her anger building more and more with each step. Marlow whined next to her, as if sensing Charly's ill feeling. Charly exhaled, trying to dispel some of the bad feelings that were moving through her. Lola hadn't really said anyone had betrayed her, but her demeanor told Charly that something was wrong.

Lola stopped. She pointed to the main house. "I saw them in there. There's a terrace level on the side. It's a wall full of windows. You can't miss them."

Charly drew her brows together. She wondered who was *them*. It was obvious that one of them was Mason, but with who and doing what? "Over there?" she asked, buying time. She was hesitant because she didn't know if she was prepared for whatever she was going to run into. She wasn't nearly as confident as she'd pretended to be with Lola. Lola nodded her head, reaching out her hand for Marlow's leash.

"Here goes nothing or everything," Charly said to herself, walking carefully and quietly to the side of the house. Passing the perfectly manicured bushes, she watched and smiled at people who decorated the lawn like weeds. They were everywhere, but what else could she expect at an outdoor party? She shook her head, trying to rid herself of the nervousness and wanting to quiet the thumping sound in her ears that was compliments of her racing heart. *Just a few feet more*, she thought, finally rounding the corner of the huge house. Then the beating in her veins stopped. And so did her breath. "Oh. No." Beside the house were Mason and Annison. They were talking and laughing, holding cups of who knew what, and looking a bit too familiar and comfortable with one another for Charly's liking. "No. No. No-no-no! What's all this about? Annison? Mason?" Charly questioned, speed-walking to where they stood. "I know y'all—"

Lola ran over and jumped in front of Charly. "Not here. Don't lose your career over this."

Charly pushed past Lola. "Annison, I know you're not trying to play me. Do you not know who I am? You may be a celebrity, but I can change all that. Not now, but right now."

Annison, still laughing, swept her hair off her bare shoulder, then locked eyes with Charly. Her smile died.

"Beat her later, Charly," Lola whispered.

Annison's eyes widened. "Charly—"

"Don't *Charly* me!" Charly snapped. She'd gotten so close to Annison that she could feel her breath bounce off Annison's face. "The minute I turn my back, you're all up in his face. Really?" She turned to Mason. "Really, Mason?"

Mason held up his hands. "Charly, calm down. It's nothing. I swear. She was just telling me how brilliant you were when you snuck on that show and pretended to be cast as a bus rider. Remember?"

Without hesitation or guilt, Annison smiled. "Charly! Hey, Charly. You're getting this all wrong. We were just laughing and celebrating you. I wouldn't do that. I'm your friend and costar. And Mason is crazy about you. But I don't need to tell you."

Mason shook his head as if disgusted with her. "I can't believe you'd accuse me."

Charly swallowed, trying to gauge her manner. She didn't know if she should be suspicious or feel silly for allowing distrust to creep in. She shook her head, feeling stupid. Mason had been nothing but good to her, and so had Annison. She had, after all, requested Charly be on the show, hadn't she? Charly spread her lips into a smile and paused, waiting for Mason to look at her. His eyes would tell her if they were being honest or not, she was sure of it. "Look at me, Mason."

He looked at her, then exhaled. She was almost sure she could see his frustration dissolve. Finally, he laughed. He turned to Annison. "Now you see why she's my girl. Charly doesn't play."

"I see. Glad you're on my side, Charly," Annison said.

Charly looked at Mason. "I'm sorry. It's just that from a distance . . ." She shook her head. It was all becoming too much. Here she was accusing her man and her costar of doing something wrong, and she blamed herself. If she hadn't been feeling the way she was about Liam, she wouldn't be distrusting Mason.

Mason smiled. "Well, if I questioned if you still cared about me or not . . ." He nodded and smiled. "You did very well in the interviews. I caught some of them." He kissed her on the cheek, then took her hand.

"Yes. I gave him an all-access pass. I thought it'd be good for him to see," Annison said, joining them. "Listen, it was good talking to you, Mason." She patted him on the back in a friendly way, almost grandmotherly like. "I'll see you guys later. I need to go chat it up with a friend," she said, then began to walk away from them. "Oh yes." She turned and paused. "Charly, thank you so much for today. You made the show interesting and fun. I'm so glad you're on it. Mason told me about you. About everything you went through to make your dreams come true. We're more alike than I knew. I don't give up or give in either," she said, then walked away, holding up her cup like she was toasting. "I hope that means that you'll finally meet us for morning yoga." Her invitation hung in the air, but Charly caught it.

Charly smiled. So she'd been wrong about Mason and Annison, and it didn't bother her like it should've. This wasn't the time to want to be right—it was the time to be sure, and she was so excited about the invite that she was even happier to be mistaken. Yes, she'd be there, but she'd keep cool about it. "So what are you drinking?" she asked.

Mason held his cup out to her, showing her there was nothing in it. "Annison gave me some nasty green healthy junk, and I poured it out. That's the other reason she was laughing so hard. No one had ever told her the drink was nasty, and she couldn't believe it. Seems she's got a lot of butt-kissers in her corner, who are too afraid to keep it one-hundred with her." He pulled her hand, and they began to walk. "I'm glad we get a little time to ourselves before I have to head over to my cousin's for the night. And I saw the perfect place for us too. There's this spot over there, surrounded by bushes and next to the water." He pointed. "If you go wait for me, I'll bring us something to drink. Maybe grab a plate. I'm starving, and I know you must be." He kissed her on the cheek.

Charly nodded, blushing. Keeping her eyes on the bench, she walked quickly toward the cozy sitting area that was a lot farther away than it had seemed. She didn't want anyone to beat her to it.

"Hey Charly! Wait!" Lola called from by the sitting area where she was standing with Sully. She walked over and grabbed Charly's arm, stopping her before she made it to the bench. "Don't trust them, Charly," she warned, keeping up with Charly's strides and pulling Marlow along. "Well, at least not her. Don't trust her. Annison can't be trusted. She was all over Mason when I saw them."

Charly stopped and looked Lola in the eyes. "All over him, like what? Touching him? Kissing him? What?"

Lola shrugged. "Well, neither one of them, really. She was just hanging a little too close to him, if you ask me, and laughing. Nothing can be that funny." She shook her head. "It appeared to be nothing, but trust me, it was everything. Flirting on top of flirting. I felt it."

Lola was being her suspicious self, reading too much into it. Charly began walking again and Lola accompanied her. The spot by the water was too comfy to let anyone beat her and Mason to it. "So they weren't doing anything? No hugging? No kissing? No touching? They were just laughing? Is that what you're telling me, Lola?" She looked over toward where the bench was and saw Sully pass the area, then another person walked near there, lingering. Charly hoped they'd keep going.

Lola rolled her eyes and reluctantly shook her head. She stopped walking. "I'm going to take Marlow and go find Sully, to give you and Mason the time alone that you need," she said to Charly's back. "But let me say this before I go: If you don't listen to me, Charly, make sure you listen to yourself. Your instinct will tell you what your mind is blocking. That girl can't be trusted." With that, Lola walked away.

The bench was set in an alcove of tall bushes, as if someone had purposely planted the greenery to surround it. The lake was off to one side of it, and a pool was directly behind it. Charly adjusted her bottom, crossed her legs, then straightened herself. She looked at the house in the distance as she settled on the bench, and thought that Mason couldn't have picked a more romantic and private place to sit—and then she changed her mind. Her eyes turned into saucers as she accidentally eavesdropped on a conversation taking place behind her, on the other side of the high bushes.

"Oh. My. Serious, Lizzy?!?" a voice asked. A voice Charly was sure could only belong to Annison. "But you're *Disney's* Lizzy. The network won't like that. So you are seeing him?"

Lizzy, one of the hugest sitcom stars on television, answered, "I am. I've been secretly dating him for months, but no one knows. We've created a pretend girlfriend for him, and you know the world thinks I'm too innocent and young to have a boyfriend. If it got out, that could cancel my contract and career." The actress exhaled. "No, it would, not could. My contract states no boyfriends until I'm seventeen—at least to the public's knowledge."

"They can do that?" Annison asked.

"Yes. Especially when you start working with them at thirteen, but they market you as a ten-year-old for the fans and merchandising. It's a kids' network. What do you expect from a network that got famous from a mouse? Everyone thinks I'm fourteen, not seventeen. He's over eighteen. So, you see how sick it could look? Promise me you won't tell a soul, Annison?" the girl whispered from the other side of the bushes. "If anyone finds this out . . ."

"You won't be able to get your own reality series. I get it. I won't tell. Promise," Annison assured her.

12

Someone was knocking on her eardrums, Charly thought, holding her head. A loud pounding echoed in the air, slicing through the quiet in the room and interrupting her rest. She grabbed the sides of her pillow and tried to fold them over her head. The banging persisted.

"What?" she yelled out.

"Yes, what!" Lola's voice cried out from the other double bed.

The banging continued. Charly's lids shot open, and her eyes found the clock. It was barely six in the morning. Her heart pounded and her adrenaline raced. She jumped off the bed, took the couple of steps to Lola's, then pulled on the sheet covering her best friend. "Get up, Lola. It must be an emergency."

Lola moaned. "If it's a fire, make sure they cremate me and finish the job."

"What?" Charly asked incredulously. "What are you talking about, Lola?"

Lola opened one eye, managing to stretch it until it was twice its normal size. "I'm not moving. I don't even care if there's an emergency because an emergency can't be as urgent as my sleep. Do you know how long I was on the phone with Sully last night?"

Charly picked up one of her pillows and tossed it at Lola's head. The banging continued. Someone was knocking on the door as if Charly's and Lola's lives depended on their answering. "Okay, okay," she said, making it to the door. "Who is it?" she asked. She may've been tired, but she was no fool. She wasn't just going to open the door without knowing who stood on the other side.

"Me, who else?" Annison's voice sang from the other side.

Charly rolled her eyes. She was sure her ears were deceiving her. "Annison?"

The door handle jiggled. "Yes. I said, let me in. It's getting late."

Charly reared back her head until it hung so far back she was sure it'd fall. Her eyes rolled and she exhaled, then grimaced. She could smell her own morning breath. "Late for what?" she asked, unlocking and opening the door.

Annison walked in all sunny and bubbly, handing her a black piece of rolled-up rubber. "Yoga. Here's your mat. I thought you said you were coming. You are joining my crew, right? I mean, you have to—you're like going to be my bestie," she said, walking to the bathroom mirror and fixing her already perfect face. "I mean, who else is confident enough and has their own career and is honest—or as Mason says, keeps it one-hundred—besides you? You're the only one I know who's like me."

Charly stretched. This was way too heavy for six in the morning. "Mm-hmm," she answered, then bumped Annison out of her way. She needed to brush fast. Overnight breath just didn't work for her.

"I'll grab you something to wear. Is your stuff still in suitcases, or did you unpack?" she asked, making her way to the sleeping area, while in the bathroom Charly tried to yell with a mouthful of toothpaste not to disturb Lola.

Chicago was beautiful in the summertime, especially by the lake, which resembled an ocean instead of an enclosed body of water. Charly looked out at the waves that seemed to go on and on. Despite being tired under an hour ago, she could appreciate the beauty and also the fresh air that blew in off the water. Marlow sat for a second, then scratched her ear.

"Where's Doll?" Charly asked Annison, who was at first reluctant about her bringing Marlow. But Marlow had to walk, and there was no way Charly was going to neglect her.

Annison's shoulders began to hunch, then she said, "She should be here. I sent one of my assistants to get her for me while I came to get you." She shook a container in her hand filled with ice and some other yucky-looking stuff, then popped it open and downed it. "Want some?

Me and the rest of the crew drink this every morning before yoga, so there's more in the cooler. I can send someone to get you one."

Charly tried to keep her expression from showing her feelings, but wasn't so successful.

"It's not that bad. You act like I offered you waste!" Annison laughed. "It's just a protein shake with egg whites added."

"Raw egg whites?" Charly had to ask.

Annison nodded. "Of course."

"No, thank you. That has salmonella written all over it. But if it works for you and the rest of the crew, have at it." Charly smiled, holding the yoga mat under her arm. It was black and heavy and smelled a little like rubber and medicine. She looked down at her clothes and felt two seconds from naked. She wore stretch pants, a fitted tank top that didn't cover anything, and flip-flops. The tights and tank were also courtesy of Annison because Charly didn't have the appropriate gear.

"It's about time! There she is, and there they are," Annison said, pointing toward a girl who was walking Doll. "You're late! And I don't do late," she yelled at the girl, then pointed to the group of yogis who were waiting on them. "Like I said at the hotel, she's going to walk Marlow too, then they can play while we do yoga. It's going to be refreshing to have class outside. I only get to do that in Cali. We always have class on the beach there."

Charly nodded, handing off Marlow to the dog walker, then rushed to catch up to Annison, who was waiting while someone unrolled her mat and adjusted it on the ground. She was in the first row, of course.

"Surya Namaskara A, then Surya Namaskara B, then fundamental Asanas. Samastitihi," the yoga instructor was saying when Charly made her way over next to Annison, rolled out her mat, and stepped out of her flip-flops.

"Huh?" she said.

Annison shook her head. "Just follow."

"Samastitihi," the instructor repeated, now walking toward Charly. "It's your starting position, Charly. Feet together, hands at your sides. Back tall. Activate your bandhas."

"She doesn't know her bandhas," Annison said.

The instructor tsked Annison. "I'll show you later, Charly," she said.

Charly frowned. "How does she know my name?" she whispered to Annison.

Annison held a finger to her lips. "Duh. You're with me, so it's her job to know. They have to know my every move. And save your breath for Vinyasa. You're going to need it. I told her you were coming. She's substituting for my private instructor who travels with me. The private instructor will have to meet you before you're allowed to come again." She shrugged. "She takes this thing too seriously, if you ask me. Get ready for Vinyasa."

Vinyasa?

"Today you'll just do the Surya Namaskaras A and B," the instructor said, passing by Charly while she went to adjust Annison's pose. "In English we call it the sun salute," she whispered. "Now exhale and fold forward, head to the knees and hands flat on the ground. Hold it. Inhale, and head up, fingertips to the ground."

Charly knew that before the morning was over, she was going to die from stretching and breathing. She wished like crazy that she could trade places with Marlow. Running next to the water seemed so refreshing.

Someone cleared their throat next to her, grabbing her attention. Charly looked to her right and didn't know whether to pass out or smile. Mason was next to her, unrolling a mat like hers. She scrunched her brows together, questioning him.

"She invited us last night, remember? Thought it would be good to watch you sweat before you leave me again. I'm missing you already." He winked.

Charly was warm, and a film of dried sweat was on her skin, but she felt good after yoga was over. Equally important, she looked good too, she noticed as she walked past a window and saw her reflection. Mason walked beside her, holding their mats and grinning. He'd had the hardest time with yoga, but he didn't give up. The instructor had told him his muscles were tight, and Charly could tell by the look on his face that the instructor's comment had been taken as a compliment, and his ego had been boosted.

"I'm glad you came out," Charly said, still a little surprised.

Mason laughed, shaking his head. "Me, miss you in that outfit? You crazy? You look good! Besides, my girl's leaving me." He leaned over and kissed her cheek. "I couldn't just let you leave without giving you something to remember."

"Hey, you two," Annison greeted them as soon as they entered the hotel. "So . . . wasn't it fabulous?"

Charly nodded. "It wasn't easy, but I have to admit, it was cool."

Mason just nodded.

"Cool enough to do it again?" Annison asked, more excited than Charly would've imagined possible after the intense workout that Annison seemed to breeze through.

Charly nodded again. "Definitely. It was hard, but my body feels good. And for some reason, I feel lighter."

Annison smiled an I-told-you-I'm-always-right smile. "Yay!" She danced in place. "Good, because that mat you have is a gift from me to you. It's a Manduka, and it will last a lifetime. I had them treat it with tea tree oil to get rid of some of the slickness; that's why it smells like that. Oh, and here," she said, handing Charly an over-sized gift bag. "Just some other essentials, like your no-skid yoga mat cover, two carriers, towels. You get it. And Mason, you can have your mat too."

Charly smiled. Annison was sweeter than she thought. "Much appreciation, Annison. Thank you so much."

"Thanks," Mason said.

"Cool. I'll see you later. I know you have to say good-bye to Mason and your other friend, wherever she is." Annison waved, then disappeared into her awaiting group of butt kissers, as Mason had called them.

Charly looked at Mason and a lump grew in her throat. Her chest rose and fell with breath warmer than usual, and she blinked slowly. "I hate good-byes," she said, feeling herself tear up. "And I can't believe I'm saying this, but I'm going to miss Illinois. You're here, and I need to check on Stormy."

"So don't say good-bye, then. You guys don't do another show for months, and Stormy is fine. You know how much of a nerd she is. Let her have her science fairs." Lola's voice came from behind. Her smile was wide, and so was Sully's, who was on her heels closer than her shadow.

"You're right. And we shoot again in weeks, barely two. Not months," Charly corrected.

Mason leaned forward, whispering in her ear. "So say you'll see us later."

13

THE EXTREME DREAM TEAM
Show 2 itinerary

Recipient information:

Deceased father victims
PLUMES, KATY & SCOTTY
Seventeen-year-old twins (female and male)
Music producers and singer/songwriters
Perform for children in hospitals and send free music to the troops.
EXTREME DREAM TEAM Mission: Design and build Katy and Scotty a music studio in their new, smaller home. They lost the other due to having to move after their father's death.
> **Charly's duties:** Assist Annison with design. Mediate between design (Annison) & carpentry (Liam). Communicate with and be responsible for recipients being away from location.

Locale: ATLANTA, GEORGIA

* * *

Where were the peaches? Charly thought, looking out of the window. She'd been looking forward to seeing fruit dangling off trees since the last show. They'd gotten a break, at least that had been the studio's plan, to give the cast some down time between shows, but anything to do with relaxing was a foreign concept to her dad. Because of him, she's sat holed up in her room, taking an online Language Arts supplementary course for a week straight, then he'd insisted she learn things she wouldn't be taught in school, namely the difference between the constitutions—plural, and she'd only been taught there was one. Though she'd been unpleased to have to study during her break, she was happy to learn something many didn't seem to know; there were actually two: The Constitution for the united states of America and THE CONSTITU-TION OF THE UNITED STATES OF AMERICA. The first was the original, the other had been adopted in 1871 and spelled in all caps, and there were clearly other differences. But she didn't want to think about government or school or anything that had to do with books now. She was free from her forced studies and was looking for fruit, the thing her mind had drifted to when she'd thought about the Peach State and how great it would be compared to studying. Charly wasn't pleased with herself, not at all. Here she was in the ATL, known as one of the hottest cities in America because of the partying, historically black colleges and universities, and multiple other reasons, she was sure, and she was still looking forward to peaches. Really? She shook her head, hoping she wasn't losing her pizzazz. Back in the day—i.e., last year—she'd have been out and about, trying to find something to do. She'd researched the city a couple of weeks ago, as soon as she'd learned they were coming. And Lola had texted her and told her to check out Lennox Square Mall, where supposedly all the rappers and singers went; Piedmont Park; and the Martin Luther King Jr. National Historic Site. She even reminded Charly of the skating rink where the movie *ATL* was filmed. Charly had promised herself that she'd have to visit at least three out of the four before she left. She couldn't be in Atlanta and leave with only fruit. That'd be lame, which she wasn't. And she definitely didn't want to do just the tourist thing either.

"We're almost there, miss," the chauffeur said, making a sharp turn on a street with the word *peach* in it, of which, Charly noticed, there were many in Atlanta.

Charly ran her hand over Marlow's tiny head, then lifted her so she could see out the window. Her tail was wagging in excitement, and Charly wished that Marlow could join her on the set. She hated to see the dogs restricted to a puppy playpen or a playroom, or worse yet, go on a walk with some unknown dog walker, who would change from location to location because the budget didn't allow for a full-time dog sitter. "Where are we?" she asked the chauffeur, who was passing a nationally known twenty-four-hour pancake house.

"We're on Peachtree. In Buckhead, miss."

Charly scrunched her nose. "Weren't we just in Atlanta? I thought we were supposed to be in Atlanta? Where did we cross the city line?" The barrage of questions flew from her mouth. She'd just been picked up from the InterContinental, which was in a ritzy section that she assumed to be downtown. They'd only driven a few blocks from the hotel, and she hadn't seen any signs indicating they were in another city.

The chauffeur laughed. "We were. We are. And we didn't, miss." He smiled, then shook his head knowingly. "You're from . . . ?" he questioned.

"I live in New York," Charly said.

He nodded. "Okay, but you don't have a New York accent," he said, shrugging. "All right, think of Manhattan. You've got Greenwich, SoHo, etcetera, but, you know, you're still in Manhattan. Same thing with Brooklyn. There's Canarsie, Bedford-Stuyvesant, Park Slope, Clinton Hill, and Fort Greene, where I'm from—"

"But it's still Brooklyn. I get it," Charly said, holding Marlow while the car pulled into a parking lot, passed a North Face store, then headed toward a Whole Foods Market that was set in the back of the lot. "I see him. He's over there," she said. "Where is everyone else?" she asked herself. Her phone vibrated in her hand. Stormy's name scrolled across the screen. "Hey! How was the science school thingy that Lola told me about. I missed you in Chicago."

"Charly, I need you to come get me. Brigette's—"

"One second, Stormy. Driver, can you stop the car for a second. I need to take this call before we pick up Liam," she said, looking at Liam in the distance. The car stopped. "Okay, Stormy. What happened?" she adjusted her wireless earpiece.

"Brigette left yesterday and there's no food here. The electric company just shut off the power, and she's not answering her phone."

Charly choked. Her mother was the worst, and Charly was too far away. "Did you call Lola?" she asked, switching phone screens. She opened her text feature and began texting Lola before Stormy could answer.

ME: 911. Stormy needs you. My mom abandoned her. No food. No power. Where r u?

LOLA: At smax's getting food. Leaving now. Tell her 2 b ready. I'm bringing BBQ.

Stormy exhaled hard. "I walked over there, but no one was home. I didn't want to call and seem like I was bothering her," she said, sounding sad.

"Get your stuff ready, Stormy. Lola's on the way," Charly said, glad that she could assist from a distance. She'd do more later, she promised herself. "She's at Smax's now, and she's bringing you some food. Text me as soon as she gets there to let me know you're all right. Okay?"

"Okay," Stormy said. Her voice was low, but lighter.

"I'll call you as soon as I'm finished taping. We're on our way to the set now, so I'm going to hang up. I don't want my costars in my business," Charly said, waving to the chauffeur that it was okay to pick up Liam now. She told Stormy she loved her, then hung up.

Liam waved with one hand and held up two brown paper shopping bags with the other in a look-what-I-have fashion. "I wasn't sure that was you because the car stopped. Seconds ago, I thought I missed you, I was in there so long," he said, opening the door before the car came to a complete stop. "This place is great! Did you know they have vegan biscuits? How do people make biscuits without eggs?" he asked, settling into the car, then bending over to give her a kiss on the cheek. The car pulled off before he sat, accidentally moving him. His lips brushed hers instead. "Sorry, love. You know that wasn't my fault, right?"

Charly smiled, brushing off the accidental kiss. She knew he didn't mean it, but the biscuit thing gave her pause for a moment. This was Liam she was talking to, and she remembered seeing on the BBC that what the British called biscuits weren't actually the same thing Americans called biscuits. It was like football and soccer. In the States football meant tackling and touchdowns, and in some places abroad, it was another word for soccer. "Biscuits?" she questioned, to be sure, then relaxed a little. Lola texted she was on her way to get Stormy.

Liam elbowed her. "Cookies. Same thing, love." He opened one of the bags and pulled out a smaller clear bag filled with a stack of cookies. "It's a six-pack of cookies. Have some? They're great, and don't worry, I got the ones made with eggs. Eggless biscuits are like flourless cakes—they both sound a little suspicious to me." He shook his head. "Weird, wouldn't you say?"

Charly laughed. Liam seemed to communicate in questions, not statements. "No, thank you. Where's Annison and Sully? I thought all of you were together. That's the message Annison left last night. She said you guys were going to the store after the yoga session and before the taping this morning." She stretched, yawning. "I just couldn't do it. I was too tired, and still am," she admitted. They'd flown in the afternoon before, gone to dinner, and Charly had been on the phone all night with Mason while the others hit the town. That was her's and Mason's usual talking schedule since they'd met up in Chicago forever ago. That's what time felt like now that they were back to being close—forever. She shook her head. She'd gone from missing him to literally counting the days they'd been apart and the days she'd have to wait to see him again.

Liam took a bite of his cookie, then closed his eyes. "Heavenly," he said, then broke off a small piece. "Taste this. You must," he demanded, pushing the cookie against Charly's lips until she opened her mouth. "Ahh, that message had to have been from last night, love. I'm assuming you didn't hear? There was no yoga this morn-ing for Annison—and yoga is girls only."

"Who says yoga is for girls?" Charly questioned. "Men do it all the time."

Liam shook his head. "If you say so. Yoga is for girls. Anyway, love, as I was saying, so there was no gym for Sully either. Seems they've both taken ill. Mr. Day said something about raw egg whites and protein and yoga." He shrugged. "Another suspicious combo if you ask me. Don't you agree?"

Charly almost swooned because his accent made it all sound sexy, then her voice caught in her throat for a sec-ond. "Wait a minute. Does that mean we're not taping?"

Liam laughed. "No, love, never that. The show must go on. Always. The network doesn't care if Annison and Sully are sick; they've already put money and time into the taping. Here," he said, then scooted to the edge of the seat and reached into his back pocket. He pulled out a folded piece of paper and handed it to Charly. "Look at that. I ran into one of the production assistants before I left the hotel. The producer or whoever will give you the updated one when we get to the set, but I thought you'd like to have a heads-up, love."

Charly unfolded the paper and saw her name typed out in bold.

REVISED (Charly)

THE EXTREME DREAM TEAM
Show 2 itinerary

Recipient information:

Deceased father victims
PLUMES, KATY & SCOTTY
Seventeen-year-old twins, female and male
Music producers and singer/songwriters
Perform for children in hospitals and send free music to the troops.
EXTREME DREAM TEAM Mission: Design and build Katy and Scotty a music studio in their new, smaller home. They lost the other due to having to move after their father's death.

Host's duties (Charly): Host the show and design rooms according to plan already in place. Communicate with Liam and his carpentry crew to complete job within allotted time limit.

Locale: ATLANTA, GEORGIA

"See, nothing changes. They've still got us."

"Do you think I can pull it off? I've never done Annison's role."

Liam shook his head. "Charly, please. You shined on the first show. Were even brighter for the cameras and interviews at the press junket, then the shows in Missouri. Did you forget about those? Us showing up to do a "pop in" at the state college was a tremendous show. Of course, you're ready."

Charly nodded, then adjusted the mic the camera crew had attached to her shirt as soon as she'd arrived on set. She wasn't giving herself enough credit. "And they keep airing commercials and clips." She smiled, giving her phone one last glance before she stepped on the set. Stormy had texted that she was with Lola, and Lola had made arrangements with her mother for Stormy to stay for awhile.

"Yes, so as I was saying," Liam said, smiling, "we're the stars today—and tonight. I hope you're ready to shine for both occasions: the reality show, and afterward the award show tonight, where we'll be making guest host appearances!"

ME: THANK U, LOLA! Guess who's hosting an award show 2nite?

*   *   *

People were everywhere. They took up almost every square foot of space that Charly could see from where she stood. Somehow the news had leaked fast, and the recipients' neighbors, family, friends, and even local pets, had all showed up for the show trying to vie for camera time, which, as far as Charly was concerned, they could have. She'd found out when she showed up to the set that the show would be airing live, and it terrified her. Live meant no room for errors. She exhaled, glad that she hadn't totally screwed up. Not yet. It would be way too embarrassing with the kazillion onlookers around who seemed to grow in numbers. The police had been called to keep the people behind the wooden barriers separating the gawkers from the crew. Charly shook her head, then snuck a wave when the camera seemed to be off her. She thought securing the area was a bit much, especially because *The Extreme Dream Team* was there to do a good deed for a couple of teenagers who lived to do the same.

"We love you, Charly," a little girl said, holding up a sign in the air that she'd probably drawn herself.

"Love you too," Charly said, then looked over one shoulder, then the other. When she saw all was clear, that no cameras were rolling, she ran across the street as fast as she could and autographed the little girl's sign, then posed for a picture with her.

The little girl screamed in glee, pointing to the ground. "Cutie. Cutie. Cutie."

Charly's gaze followed the little girl's finger, then she swallowed hard. Marlow was at her feet, moving a million miles an hour, her tiny paws scampering as her tail wagged in the air like a flag. With one scoop, Charly had Marlow in her arms. "How'd you get out?" she asked, looking around for Marlow's sitter.

"Can I pet her?" the little girl asked, reaching out her hand over the barrier.

Charly grinned, then leaned on the barrier so the little girl could reach Marlow. "This is Marlow, my puppy . . ." Her words trailed off when she noticed two things that told her the crew was done cleaning and setting up the recipients' new spaces. One, a cameraman had his lens pointed at her and Marlow and the little girl. Two, a producer was rotating his index finger in the air in small circles while mouthing, *Keep going. It's good. Really good.*

It was great—super great, Charly thought, not believing her luck. She felt bad for Annison, and wouldn't have wished sickness on anyone, but she'd be a liar if she didn't admit to loving the leading role and spending time with the recipients. The closer it came to wrapping the show, the more she grew to love it. The spotlight held so much more for her than just the opportunity to shine the brightest; it gave her confirmation that she'd done the right thing by going after her dream. And it couldn't get any better. Even without Annison, the show was proving to be a success, just as she and Liam were. They worked effortlessly together, easing into one scene after another as if they'd been reading from a script. But there was no script, not in black and white. Yet something was definitely scripted in the universe for them. Something magical that Charly wanted to deny, but couldn't. By the way Liam kept looking at her, Charly realized he also must've felt what she did.

"Until next time, we'll see you later," Liam said into the camera.

"And who knows?" Charly began, spreading her smile wider than any beauty pageant contestant. "We may just end up in your neighborhood. Remember, if you know someone who's fantastically fabulous, needs our help, and deserves an *Extreme Dream Team* makeover, let us know. That's what we're here for. Until then . . ." Charly finished, waving to the camera.

"Now, that was a beautiful wrap, Charly, my love!" Liam said, winking. "On par with the makeover we just completed, and just as well deserved!" He blew her a kiss, then the lights on the camera died, signaling it was off.

Charly's gown was gorgeous. "Perfect," she said aloud, turning in front of the mirror. White silk wrapped her body like a second skin, making her caramel complexion seem to glow. "Whaddya think?" she asked, slowing her spin in front of the computer monitor so Lola, Stormy and Mason could see. They'd all gathered at Mason's to help her get ready via Skype.

"You. Look. Good!" Mason complimented. Flirtation and pride laced his voice.

"Beautiful," Stormy sang. "Wow, Charly, I always said you were pretty, but I didn't know you were like Tyra Banks *America's Top Model* pretty."

"Get 'em, girl. Get 'em, girl. Get 'em!" Lola yelled. "Bang 'em out, Charly. They're not even going to see you coming."

Charly spun one more time. "I know, right? I got this.

I got this. I'm gonna make y'all so proud. Wait and see."
She cleared her voice. "Good evening, ladies and gentle-
men, My name is Charly St. James—Charly with a Y!"
she laughed, pretending to have a mic in front of her.
"But for real, on the up and up, I'm mad nervous. I got
the crazy shakes inside." She sat on the edge of the chair,
where she could still see the computer monitor.

"Let me tell you something, baby. There's no need to
be nervous. You're gonna kill 'em with your talent and
beauty. You hear me?" Mason questioned.

Charly nodded.

"Yes, sis. You'll do well. You always do. That's why
I'm so proud of you, Charly. You never give up," Stormy
said, her face now a little too close to the computer camera.

"Thank you again, Lola. I owe you, and I love you
guys!" She looked at the clock on the nightstand. "I gotta
go. There's only minutes to show time."

"Love you too," Lola spoke. "And you don't owe me."

"I love you," both Mason and Stormy said in unison.

"Wish me luck, we're getting ready to go on. Live!"
she said, her heart making its way up in her chest with
just the thought as she ended the video chat.

Charly's hand was on the doorknob, but she couldn't
turn it. Her life had changed in a major way, and she was
happy. Almost completely happy. She'd captured her
dream, and now she was truly on her way. She had the
reality series and, now, was hosting an award show. The
only thing left for her to do was to make sure Stormy was
all right, and not for a few days, but forever. She inhaled
deeply, held her head high, then reminded herself of who

she was. She was Charly St. James, and she could conquer the world, that's what she told herself as she finally opened the door so she could go meet Liam.

Liam ran his hand over his wet hair, then shook it, making water fly like droplets of summer rain. He'd been running late, and was now barely dressed. He slid into his tuxedo jacket, buckled the buckle on his dark jeans, then bent over and adjusted the laces on his nineteen-eighties shell-toe Adidas sneakers. Charly swallowed her admiration, and would've kicked herself for taking in his every move, but she couldn't help it, and had been enjoying watching him finishing dressing so much, she'd have done it twice. She was thankful that she'd made it to meet him when she did. If she'd made it to meet him two minutes later, she'd have missed him getting ready.

He licked his lips, then ran his index finger over the corners of his mouth, spreading the moisturizer he'd used. "Not too much, right, love? I don't want to be on film looking like a girl. Glossy lips aren't masculine," he said, then turned Charly's way. He wiped his hands on a towel, then reached out and fixed her hair.

Warmth climbed her neck, making her rear back. She nodded. "Um. Yes. I mean, no. Your lips are just fine," she said, but thought, *perfectly kissable fine*. She kept nodding her head and couldn't seem to stop.

"Nervous, love?" he asked, smiling.

Charly nodded. "Yes." She laughed, knowing she must look silly.

"Five minutes," a producer for a major entertainment network announced to them, splaying his index and middle fingers into a V.

"Ready," she said, then took her spot next to Liam on the red carpet, looked at the teleprompter she'd be reading from, and told herself to prepare. She was a reality show star this morning. Tonight she was a celebrity host at an award show that was being broadcast live all over America and in certain parts of the globe.

"You're not ready yet, love," Liam said and grabbed her around the waist, bent her backward and planted the sweetest, softest kiss on her lips, then brought her to her feet. "I'd say that now you are, definitely!" He licked his lips, then made a smacking noise. "And delicious too, I must say. You are ready. You, me, and the rest of the world. Welcome everyone to the award show of all award shows. I'm Liam," he said to the camera, then held out his hand to Charly. "And this is Charly St. James, my costar with the most kissable lips in the world. And now that we've got that out of the way, let me tell you what we've got in store for you tonight . . ."

Oh God. The whole world was watching.

14

"I didn't know he was going to kiss me! It was only for the camera, trust me. All publicity," Charly yelled into the suite's phone, pacing back and forth in the hotel room. "The kiss was scripted . . . for him and Annison. Yes, I'm sure," she lied without effort. "He wasn't supposed to kiss *me*—he was supposed to kiss *whoever*. Annison, I guess. And *whoever* just happened to be me because I was filling in for her. She was sick, so I had to cover for her twice. Once for *The Extreme Dream Team*, and then I had to do the award show that you're so upset about," she tried to explain, but her father wasn't believing her story.

Her cell vibrated in her other hand, and she shook her head, looking at the text. Both of the guys in her life were acting up, and it was killing her. Movie stars performed all the time for the cameras, so what was so wrong with her and Liam sharing a little smooch? It was lip service only, no French kiss, she'd told both her father and her boyfriend, Mason, but for some reason, neither cared. Now her father wanted to come get her and take her with him to some military base he had to go to, and Mason's texts were filled with accusations. Charly had tried to convince him that there was nothing between her and Liam, but try as she might, she saw there was no winning with either of them. Their minds were made up, but so was hers, and she wasn't wrong. So there was no point arguing anymore.

"That was days ago, Dad. I'm not in Atlanta anymore. I'm in Miami now. I just got into my room under an hour ago. And, no, you can't just come get me. We have a show to do here, and you signed a contract, remember? Not to mention, you just said you had to go away for . . . ?"

"Nine days, Charly. The weekend, then Monday through Saturday," he snapped.

Charly exhaled and rolled her eyes while her father continued to yell into the phone that he didn't care about a piece of paper, that he felt as if the studio had been keeping him in the dark about her schedule, and how she was to stay over at her aunt's while he was away—he threatened to check—then stated that no one could tell him what he could and could not do about his daughter. She winced, his loudness penetrating her eardrums as if he were trying to burst them. "Language, Dad. Language! Please? I can't do this now. I gotta get Stormy settled—she's with Lola because Brigette left again. So just think, some things are bigger than me and you. Consider that, please?" she begged, almost disbelieving that her father and Mason knew so many curse words. She was almost glad she didn't have to host again with Liam, just so she could make her dad and Mason feel better. But *almost* was the key word. She loved hosting, and the truth was, she'd do it again in a heartbeat. She'd take their attitudes and foul language and accusations all over again, and not just for the camera time, but for the company too. Liam had been great to look at and work with. "I love you, Dad. I love you. And don't worry while you're away. Just enjoy your work and relax. I'm sure Annison is better by now, so I won't be with Liam so much. My focus is helping Annison and the recipient, remember?" She paused, waiting to hear something else negative, but was met with pure silence. "I have to go. Gotta be on the set immediately," she lied, then hung up.

Charly's stomach knotted, making her wince. A loud rumble announced itself, reminding her she hadn't eaten since the day before, but food would have to wait. She looked at her phone, and cringed. Lola had texted that some agency had been driving by their house looking for Stormy and Brigette. A neighbor had told her. A gut feeling told her that even though her sister was bunking over at Lola's, something was very wrong in her sister's world— that there was something terrible brewing. And the agency, who Charly believed was social services or something, made it worse. Who else would come looking for Stormy? she wondered. If the people were just looking for her mother, that'd be different. But what agency would look for a child? School was out, and Stormy had never been truant, so Charly was just about sure it was social services. Lola had said she'd seen them before—the same two agents—pick up a child near her. Biting her lip,

Charly scrolled through her text messages, searching for someone—anyone—who could help. She exhaled in frustration, running her fingers through her hair. There was no one. Brigette, their mother, was to blame for all the madness. Why couldn't she just be a good, normal mom like most mothers? She couldn't have anyone put her sister into the foster system. That was the last thing she needed now, not when her life was changing—and changing it was. On the one hand, her star was rising. Taking Annison's place had made her feel good and let her know that she was capable of having her own show. On the other hand, her world as she knew it was crashing. Her dad was irate. Mason's boxer shorts seemed to be in a twist because he had a straight attitude that Charly felt she didn't deserve. And now, the closest she could get to Stormy was phone or Skype conversation.

"Knock. Knock." Liam's voice sounded through the door, penetrating Charly's thoughts and the silence of the hotel room.

Charly was caught off guard by Liam's popping up. She knew he couldn't hear her thoughts, but she felt like someone had been eavesdropping. "One second," she yelled toward the door, then did a double take, checking herself in the mirror. As suspected, she looked tired, but she didn't care. She was tired from traveling, exhausted from going back and forth with her dad and Mason, and was comfortable enough with Liam to let him see her as she was. That's what she told herself, then changed her mind, fixing her hair while she went to let him in. "Hey," she greeted, stepping back and allowing him entrance.

"Good day, love," he said, purposely turning up his accent to make Charly smile.

Her stomach growled her reply.

Liam laughed. "Well, that answers my question then." He pointed to her midsection. "I was coming to see if you'd like to grab a bite. Seems like you do."

Charly looked at the clock on the nightstand. She'd missed breakfast time. Her stomach rumbled again, this time longer and louder. "I really can't, Liam. I have to get to my sister . . . she's sorta my responsibility. For most of our lives, all we've had is each other."

Liam's eyes widened and he nodded knowingly. He clasped his hands together in front of him and pressed his lips together. "Well, love, that's understandable. I don't really get it, but you can explain while we eat. As much as you want to drop everything—including eating—you really can't. How are you going to help your sister if you're hungry? No food means no energy." He laced his arm through hers, then pulled her toward the door, stopping by the closet. "Step into your shoes or I'm taking you outside in your bare feet."

Charly stuffed her feet into a pair of ankle boots, then bent over to lace the right one. "So I missed yoga? I assumed we'd have a late session, and I wanted to go." She moved her fingers to the other foot, then tied the left bootie. "Where are we eating?" She whistled Marlow over and put on her leash. "Wherever it is, Marlow is coming or we're sneaking her in." She walked over to the closet, then on tiptoes she stretched to grab a dog carrier that resembled a large tote.

"We—meaning just me and you and Marlow—are eating somewhere within walking distance, hopefully."

A knock sounded on the door. "Charly?" a voice called. "This is for you."

Liam opened the door. "Ahh, thank you. Do you have my copy too?" He reached into the hallway, then seconds later closed the door. "A production assistant with the itinerary. Here, this is your copy." He handed Charly the slip of paper.

THE EXTREME DREAM TEAM
Show 3 itinerary

Recipient information:

Animal rescuer
DAVIS, DEMY
Fourteen-year-old female
Dog lover, humanitarian
Rescues animals from kill shelters and finds them homes.
EXTREME DREAM TEAM Mission: Design and build Demy an indoor-outdoor shelter, complete with dog runs, bathing area, play area, and lodging.

> **Host's duties (Charly):** Host the show, and design rooms according to plan already in place. Communicate with Liam and his carpentry crew to complete job within allotted time.

Locale: MIAMI, FLORIDA

He rocked back and forth from his toes to his heels. "You really need to talk to Mr. Day more, love. He said the ratings are through the roof, and because Annison and Sully are still victims of their food choices—who eats raw eggs after the discovery of salmonella, anyway?—it's just us again."

Charly's eyes widened. "Really? I'm hosting again? But how? Annison and Sully can't still be sick, and aren't they here or supposed to be here by now? And we don't do the show for a couple of days, right?"

Liam nodded and opened the door for her. "I already knew about the change, and I was getting ready to tell you just before the production assistant came. I just hung up with Annison before I knocked on your door. They aren't sick. Because they got food poisoning, the higher ups want them to be tested for food allergies or something like that. They need to be cleared to work by a doctor." He shrugged. "So, yes, it's just us again as long as you bring Marlow on the set. I guess the viewers really took to you and Marlow, because ratings were higher on the last show compared to when Annison was hosting."

The diner was situated on the corner between two other buildings as if someone had dropped it there. It wasn't centered and it wasn't constructed of the same materials as the other buildings, but looked like it was part trailer, part outdoor cafeteria, and part corner store. Charly stroked Marlow, making her comfortable in the tote, then hoisted the carrier higher on her shoulder to prevent anyone from eyeing the dog.

"Well, we wouldn't have to worry about anyone hearing Marlow if she did whine, would we, love?" Liam asked.

Charly shook her head, then smiled and bopped to the loud Spanish music that wafted through the air along with the aroma of strong coffee, which was being served in tiny cups at a station with a CAFÉ sign above it. Another counter was surrounded by mostly construction men and one or two teenagers. Charly nodded toward the line of people waiting for their dark-liquid fix, then moved her gaze over by the men who wore white overalls with paint splattered on them.

"Definitely Miami," she said to Liam, craning her neck. She was trying to see through the lunch crowd that had beaten them inside. "I wonder what's the big deal at that counter?" She pointed.

Liam grinned, then grabbed her hand. He pulled her through the crowd in front of them and pointed toward the opposite corner. "Go grab us a seat over there before they're all taken, and I'll show you what all the fuss is about at that counter, love. It's more than a huge deal— trust me."

Charly nodded, then excused herself as she tried to make her way to the other side of the restaurant, walking as slow as she could to see what was going on at the counter.

"See," Liam said, pointing. "It's the coffee. Cuban espresso and Cuban sandwiches. There's nothing like them, that's why the counter is so busy."

Charly smiled, and patted her stomach. She couldn't

wait to try the Cuban sandwich. If they were good enough to have the people lined up and making a fuss, she had to have one. She made her way to an empty booth. Her head nodded and her feet tapped, feeling the sexy rhythm of the music. She had no idea what they were singing about, and didn't understand more than a word or two of Spanish, but the song was fantastic. "Sorry," she said, bumping into a waitress, who returned her apology with a smile. Bypassing the worker, Charly slid around her and spotted various newspapers scattered on the unoccupied table. A celebrity-gossip tabloid caught her attention, and she grabbed it before sitting in the adjacent empty booth and setting her cell phone on the table. "Oh . . ." Her mouth dropped, leaving the vowel sound hanging in the air as she tried to blink her disbelieving eyes. "It can't be." Her head shook in the negative. She didn't want to believe what she was seeing, but it was there scrawled across the paper in all capital letters and underlined in red.

FOURTEEN-YEAR-OLD LIZZY DATING GROWN MAN? (Insider gives the full story on page 2.)

Charly's nails almost broke trying to turn the page as quickly as her trust in Annison was dissolving. She swallowed, feeling bad for Lizzy. Lizzy was the hugest teen celebrity there was, and now, because of Annison, Charly was sure Lizzy's star was falling fast and hard. There was no denying it or lying to herself, not after she read, almost verbatim, the words Lizzy had confided in Annison that night when Charly overheard them talking in Chicago, while she sat on the other side of the bush.

"I've been secretly dating him for months, but no one knows. We've created a pretend girlfriend for him, and you know the world thinks I'm too innocent and young to have a boyfriend. If it got out, that could cancel my contract and career. He's over eighteen. So, you see how sick it could look? If anyone finds this out . . ."

". . . your career is over," Charly said, finishing what Lizzy was implying, then moved her eyes to her cell phone, which had begun vibrating on the table, signaling a text.

MASON: only act together? yeah rite! well y was Liam in ur hotel room?

Charly gulped, shook her head, and rolled her eyes. How did Mason know Liam had stopped by her room? She knew for a fact without knowing for a fact, she told herself, the whole knowing without knowing making sense to her. Annison had something to do with Mason's knowing about her being with Liam. He'd told he he'd just spoken to Annison earlier, and her best friend, Lola, had urged her to listen to her instincts, hadn't she? Charly nodded, answering her own question and remembering Lola's warning about Annison: *That girl can't be trusted.*

REMEMBERING WHERE YOU CAME FROM

15

"ACTION! Final scene!" the director yelled.

Charly inhaled. She'd done everything she was supposed to, and had done it well. She'd smiled the whole time. Performed for the cameras. Enjoyed designing and decorating Demy Davis's dream haven for the dogs she rescued from kill shelters. She worked well with the recipient of *The Extreme Dream Team*, and loved the likeminded girl's company so much she'd found a food sponsor that would feed Demy's rescue dogs for a year. Still, something was off. Charly nodded, still grinning like she'd won something, but inside she was livid. The camera followed her every move, a thing she would normally have loved and had dreamed about forever, but now she hated it because it felt as if it was suffocating her. What she needed now was time alone to process what Annison had done and what she knew the mega actress Lizzy was going to have to endure.

"Almost there, love," Liam whispered to her through clenched teeth while they waved good-bye to the cameras, finally wrapping up the show.

"And that's a wrap!" the director sang, swirling his hand in the air.

"Great!" Charly said, the fake smile still plastered across her face even after the red recording light on top of the camera signaled they were done.

"So you're just going to stand here?" Liam asked, walking away. "We're done, you know?"

Charly gulped and tried to loosen up. "I'm going to do much more than that," she said.

"This is for you, Charly. The itinerary, and there's a message for you there too," a producer said, handing Charly a light blue piece of paper with the word *Memo* on top.

Charly gave it a quick glance, then folded it and put it in her back pocket. "Thanks. I'll get on whatever it is as soon as I can," she said.

"I appreciate it. The way I was rushed, I'm under the impression it's kind of important."

Charly smiled to appease the producer, but in reality she wasn't the happy girl her smile showed her to be. In fact, her shoulders tensed over the memo. Her father had threatened to come get her, and now she was sure Mr. Day wanted to talk to her about the kiss she and Liam shared—the kiss that really had nothing to do with Mr. Day or *The Extreme Dream Team*. She grimaced. It was all becoming too much—her dad, Mason, Stormy, being accused of being with Liam, Annison, and poor Lizzy being splashed across a tabloid—and Charly was getting tired of it. She wanted to bust. After she'd read the gossip magazine, she swallowed the information and didn't tell Liam what had happened. Instead, she'd flipped the magazine over. She didn't want to add to the messiness of Lizzy's situation or the probability that Annison was purposely destroying Lizzy's career. And it was killing her. She now needed to talk, but didn't know who she could trust. She was surrounded by actors, so how was she to know if the people around her were really her friends, or just acting like it, like Annison had done with Lizzy? She exhaled, then removed the memo from her pocket. She couldn't let a thing like words from her dad or Mr. Day make her nervous. She wasn't afraid of anything. Unfolding the blue memo sheet, she decided to deal with all the things that made her tense at once. Then she hated that she did. It was a message from Stormy sent through Lola's phone.

I left Lola's house. I heard her mom fussing and saying we were eating up all the food. I'm going back home. I'll be okay.—Stormy

"Liam, when do we leave Miami?" *I need to go home to Illinois. ASAP.*

Liam shrugged. "I don't know, but we're set to do Virginia Beach next. Why?" he asked, pulling out his phone to check his calendar. He touched a few spots on his touch screen. "I took a picture of the itinerary and saved it in my pictures. I just forwarded it to so you can save it in your cell. Now there's no excuses, love." He winked.

"Thanks. I already got a copy from the producer, but I didn't look at it. And don't ask why." Charly whipped out her phone, selected her favorites, and searched for Lola's name. Without looking up, she organized her next few days. "Liam, can you keep Marlow for me for a day or so? I have some urgent business that I need to sneak to Illinois to handle. And I can't let my dad or Mr. Day know what's up. Please?" she asked while she sent a text into the universe.

> on my way 2 illinois tmrw. Stormy's at our house. Crash @ ur place?

She received a response almost immediately.

> LOLA: yay! & yep
> p.s. the Sully dude is a flake.

The Illinois sidewalks felt different under her feet, Charly thought, walking with Lola toward her old home. She waved to a couple of neighbors, who'd strained their eyes hard enough to make her out in the dim light the streetlight provided and made it their business to tell her how glad they were to be her friend, even though before she'd been on television they'd never spoken to her a day in her life. Charly plastered on a fake smile and thanked them while she multitasked and called her mother's house again. She knew no one was going to answer because the number had been disconnected, but she had to try anyway. It wasn't unlike their mother to pay to get the service reconnected in a matter of hours after the phone was shut off.

"No luck," she said as the few cracked cement steps that led to the house's walkway crunched under her feet.

She looked at the plain-looking place she'd once called home, though it had never felt like it. Cars zoomed down the block, most having seen better days and others blasting music like they were equipped with club speakers. Charly shook her head. The state of the automobiles, people, and fractured sidewalks were telltale signs of what kind of place she'd been raised in, and she was thankful to be out. The town was boring for a teenager. The neighborhood was a little less than middle class, but livable. Her mother, Brigette, was the opposite of a caring, supportive parent. "Whatever." She dismissed the bad things, then refocused on her sister. She ascended the porch stairs, pulled open the battered screen door, and saw there was a new lock on the door. "Guess that means using my key is out of the question," she said, raising her brows in surprise. She wondered when the locks had been changed, then knocked on the hollow door.

"I told you, I haven't seen her," Lola reported, two steps behind Charly. "I came by here earlier. No one came to the door, but I think someone was in the house. And every time I call her, I get voice mail, just like you. Sometime it rings, sometimes it just goes straight to voice mail."

Charly nodded, ignoring the cell vibrating in her pocket. "It shouldn't be. I paid her bill months ahead with my first check." The phone danced again, wiggling against her hip. She knew it had to be her dad or Mr. Day, who'd probably discovered that she'd caught the first thing flying to Chicago—or at least must've been suspicious about why she was missing. It could also be her aunt, who was expecting Charly when she returned from Miami. Charly walked down the porch stairs, putting her hands on her hips and looking around the yard that was barely visible in the darkness. "What made you think someone was here?"

Lola shrugged. "I could just tell. I didn't hear a TV or anything like that because the power is off, as you already know, but I knew. Just like I know Sully is a flake. Did I tell you that?"

Charly nodded. "You did. Three times before I made it out of the airport, four times while I was in the cab on the way over here," she said, hoping Lola would take the hint that now wasn't a good time to talk about Sully or anything else besides finding Stormy.

"Did I tell you he has a girlfriend?"

Charly shook her head. *"Really?"* Her question was dry. "Can you tell me about it later, Lola? I need to concentrate." She exhaled her frustration into the Illinois breeze and pressed her lips together in thought. If Stormy wasn't inside, Charly had no idea where she could be. Her sister was a nerdy loner who had no friends except Charly. "Got an idea." She walked to the side of the house, waving her hand for Lola to follow, then rounded toward the back of the house, submerging herself in almost complete darkness. "If you can't find a way, make a way," she whispered, then froze. Her phone was vibrating again. "Stop calling already," she hissed.

"Just answer it," Lola mumbled. "I don't see what the big deal is. Who can prove you're out of town, anyway? You didn't tell anyone," she deadpanned. It was a statement, not a question.

"Just Liam. I had to have someone watch Marlow and

cover for me. And before you say it, Lola, yes, I can trust him. Whoever it is—my dad or Mr. Day, I'll just tell them I'm having female problems and I'm in my room and don't want to be disturbed. There's not a man around who wants to hear that. And if it's my aunt, she should understand." Charly laughed, carefully walking the few steps to the back porch. She pulled her phone from her pocket and touched the screen to make it light. Her eyes widened. It wasn't Mr. Day or her father calling. It was Mason. "Yes, Mason?" she answered, prepared for more attitude from him. She climbed the back porch stairs, pulled open the torn screen door, and tried the doorknob. Her eyebrows shot up toward heaven. The door wasn't locked.

"One sec," she said to Mason, then used her phone as a flashlight, turning it toward Lola, who held up her thumb. "Go in. Go in!" Lola urged, her whisper low but clear.

Charly turned the knob all the way until she heard it click, then she pushed open the door. "Yes," she mouthed.

A scream cut through the air. A stick cracked against her wrist. Lola's body was pressed against her back, trying to help her push all the way inside the house, then suddenly she was doing the opposite; her hands were on Charly, trying to pull her out of the doorway. "What in the—?" Lola yelled.

The person inside the house, who Charly assumed and hoped was Stormy, grabbed one of Charly's wrists with two hands, then began twisting her wrist as if trying to break it while kicking at her with one foot.

"Get out! Get out or I'm going to break your wrist," Stormy said, then screamed again, loud and shrill.

Charly froze for a split second. "Stormy? Stormy, is that you? It's me. Charly!"

"Charly?" Stormy said.

16

It was a mess. What their excuse for a mother had done to Stormy was a certifiable disaster, and Charly was beyond peeved. Stormy was barely fourteen. How could Brigette just leave her? Charly wondered as she sat crosslegged, bopping her leg back and forth at a small table at her old workplace, Smax's BBQ. She was trying to curb her anger, answer the questions Stormy couldn't, and come up with a plan while Stormy and Lola ate like they hadn't had a meal in years. Charly grimaced. She could tell it had been a while since her little sister had had a decent meal because she refused to eat as much as usual at Lola's out of politeness, but Lola, she knew, was just plain greedy.

"Stormy, why did you just leave? Lola's mom always fusses. She doesn't mean anything. She's been fussing at me and Lola forever. You should've said something. Why didn't you?" she asked, knowing what her sister would say before she said it. Their mother had trained them both well, and the first thing she'd taught them was to keep their mouths shut. You never put your family's business or your feelings in the street.

"What was I supposed to say, Charly? And *why* would I say anything?" Stormy questioned. "Brigette leaves us alone all the time, so what was so different this time, besides you not being here?" She shrugged. "Plus, I can't find my phone. I brought it to the house with me, then it was gone. I took a nap, woke up, and poof. It was out of there. And Lola did a lot for me. I didn't want to keep intruding on them. And, even if I had my phone, I wouldn't have called you because you're on the road. And when haven't we been able to fend for ourselves?" Stormy looked at Lola and gave her a half smile. "No offense, Lola. I appreciate what you did."

Charly shot Stormy a look. "Brigette must have it. She's the master of sneaking in and taking your stuff, then sneaking out. She used to do that to me all the time. Tell me why you left Lola's again. It doesn't make sense."

"All right. All right." Stormy rolled her eyes. "I didn't tell Lola I was leaving because I didn't want to bother you, and Lola would've told. We both know that Lola can't hold water," Stormy continued, then turned to Lola. "I hope you don't take offense," Stormy apologized, then turned back to Charly. "Plus, I wanted you to enjoy your dream, Charly. Not check on me every five minutes."

Lola smiled. "No offense taken," she said matter-of-factly.

Charly jumped in. "Okay. Okay. I get it. Are you sure

you have no idea where Brigette is, Stormy? I still can't believe she left you," she began, then remembered who they were discussing. She bopped her head. As irritated as she was, she couldn't help but groove to the crazy remix of Marvin Gaye, Parliament, and Sly and the Family Stone that blared from grease-laden speakers that were visibly wired to the stand in the corner where DJ the deejay spun real vinyl records. "On second thought, I take that back. Yes, I can. I can believe she left you. I just wish you had called me before you left Lola's. I was scared to death, Stormy." She rapped her knuckles on the table, keeping time with the bass line. If her having an old soul was ever in question when she'd worked at Smax's, it wasn't in question anymore. She was definitely an old soul trapped in a young body, and current music didn't move her the way the classics did.

Stormy set her corn on the cob down on her plate, then pushed up her glasses on her nose with the side of her hand. She sucked her teeth in irritation. "I told you I couldn't, Charly."

"That's right. Your phone's missing."

"*Missing?* Yeah, right. You just said you believe Brigette has it, and so do I," Lola interrupted, wiping barbecue sauce from the corners of her mouth. "That's why it rings sometimes, and other times it doesn't. She ignores our calls or sends them to voice mail or powers off the phone."

Charly nodded, looking toward the door. Mason was supposed to meet her but hadn't shown yet. They'd been at Smax's for almost an hour, more than enough time for him to get there. She looked at her cell to see if he'd texted, but he hadn't. The last thing she needed was to worry about Mason while she was trying to figure out what to do about Stormy, she told herself, but she couldn't get him out of her head. He'd been so mad at her lately, and she hadn't done anything wrong. Sure, she could understand him not liking that Liam kissed her, but that wasn't her fault. She hadn't kissed him back, but she hadn't pulled away either. That had been Mason's argument, and she knew he had a point.

The bell over the restaurant entrance rang, pulling Charly's attention. A girl walked in, and Charly's heart dropped from disappointment. Where was he? She'd told him she had a problem, had given him as much information as she could in the few minutes she'd spoken to him, and he'd stood her up. Charly reached for her cell phone, throwing her ego to the wind, then sent him a text asking where he was.

"Charly? *Charly?* Is that you? You musta come in here when I was in the back with Smax. There's no other way I woulda missed you. Not my Charly! Heard you on television now, huh? Big star!" Rudy-Rudy-Double-Duty, the self-nicknamed double war vet who'd been patronizing Smax's since it opened its doors, winked, then smiled, diverting her attention from waiting on Mason to reply to her text.

Charly smiled, glad to see Rudy-Rudy. He'd been one of Charly's favorites when she lived in Illinois. "Hey, Rudy-Rudy! I missed you too!" Charly yelled from her seat, a genuine smile coming over her face and shedding a little brightness on her gloomy mood. "I'll be over there in a minute, okay?"

"Okay. Make sure too, because I need to know where

ya been all my life. You know nobody can slice corn bread like you. And that's why I ain't had a piece since you left," he teased while biting into a corn muffin, the only other bread Smax served besides dinner rolls.

"Charly, my dear? That *is* you, I was sitting in my car taking a call and thought I saw you, but wasn't sure," Dr. Deveraux El said, walking in. "It certainly is good to see you. I see the moon and stars—Ursa Minor and Ursa Major—or one of them, obviously, served you well," he said, looking like his usual dapper self. "As you see, I've been studying," he pointed to the bar where his papers were spread out next to a globe. He pulled a compass out of his pocket, then a pencil.

Charly smiled big and wide. She apologized to Rudy-Rudy for making him wait, then stood up and walked over to Dr. Devereux El. She embraced him. "Thank you so much, Dr. Deveraux El. If it weren't for you, who knows where I'd be? I'd probably still be in the middle of nowhere or worse, like on the side of the road. You saved me. You and your moon-and-stars information—all this," she said, pointing to his spread. "Yes, because of you, I became a little Harriet Tubman and used the stars to find my way to a gas station. My costar from the show was there," she said, referring to the night the bus had broken down and accidentally left her and Marlow. Dr. Deveraux El had saved her life and her career, as far as she was concerned.

He patted her back. "Deveraux, Charly. Remember, just call me Deveraux." Dr. El nodded, then picked up a cup of tea and held it up as if toasting her. His pinky finger was still in the air when she finally released him. "It was my pleasure and duty, Charly. We're all supposed to uplift others—help them find their way. I only gave you what your ancestors gave us, Charly. Light. And that light brought you home." His words explained, but the brightness behind his eyes said he was proud and genuinely cared—something Charly was sure he'd never express verbally. Dr. Deveraux El was all intellect, and never personal.

Charly smiled and nodded. They'd gone through the same Dr. Deveraux El versus Just call me Deveraux at least twice a week when she'd worked at the restaurant. She'd always address him as Doctor and he'd always corrected her. If only Dr. Deveraux El hadn't had such a superior air, she would've called him by his first name. "Okay, sir. I mean Deveraux. Oh, by the way. I now know there are two constitutions. I've been studying," she said with pride.

"Good for you, Charly. Now study the Magna Carta and Daughters of the Revolution. I think you'll be surprised."

Charly smiled. "I will Dr. Deveraux. And my thanks to you again. If it weren't for you—"

He smiled, shushing her. "No. I have nothing to do with nature's laws or universal law, remember. You are what you were supposed to be. Now, if you want to thank me, learn about universal law—it's the only law there is."

"Charly! Charly, gal. Is that you? I thought I heard your voice," Smax, the owner, greeted as he strode through the double doors that led to the kitchen. "Bathsheba! Sheba, come out here. Charly's home!"

Charly looked at Smax and grinned so hard her cheeks hurt. After all the tension she'd had in a day, Smax was a sight for sore eyes. Barely four-eleven, he wore his gray hair in long finger waves, and his thick mustache was curled up and over at the ends like rams' horns. His smile was literally glowing: both his front teeth, spaced wide apart, were outlined by gold crowns with diamonds in the center. Today he wore lemon-yellow alligator shoes and a matching three-piece suit with a purple shirt underneath. Charly's eyes moved to the coat rack in the rear, and, sure enough, an equally bright banana-colored Dobbs hat hung there. Finger waves or no, Smax wouldn't be caught dead without a coordinating brim to match his outfit.

"Hey, Smax!" Charly greeted. "Sorry I didn't come straight to the back to say hello. I had some business to take care of first—including paying for our food," she said, motioning her head toward Stormy and Lola. "You hired a nice girl to replace me too."

Smax nodded, removing a custom-made gold toothpick from his mouth. He glanced at the clock, then at Charly. "Yeah, I guess." He paused and looked around. "Wait a minute. Did you say *pay*? You paid for the food?" He shook his head. "You know you didn't have to do that, Charly. You're family, and you were always on time when you worked here. But that new girl? Now, *she*'s always late."

Charly put a hand on her hip. "Smax, remember you said the same thing about me!" She laughed.

"And me! He says the same thing about me, but I'm the one who wakes him up in the morning," Bathsheba,

Smax's common-law wife, boomed as she pushed her way through the double doors, then barreled her way over to Charly and embraced her in a bear hug, almost drowning her with her huge bosoms. "Charly. I missed you." She pecked Charly on the cheek. "Now come on, tell Momma Bathsheba, why you really here? I know my Charly, so I know something ain't right. You didn't just bust through these doors without giving some type of notice first. Stars," she said, pinching Charly's cheek as if she were a baby. "Meaning you don't just pop up, especially when you wanted to get away so badly."

Smax nodded at Charly, winking twice. "Yessir, we know you, just like I know that big-head girl over there ain't gone never pay for her food or run outta room for my spareribs," he said, sounding like he was joking, but he wasn't. Smax never joked about Lola and her eating, especially because she ate at his restaurant for free, due to rumors he was her real father.

Lola waved her hand at Smax, dismissing him while she bit into a saucy rib. Though chewing, she still managed to sneer at him. She pointed at Charly. "She paid."

Smax sucked on his teeth as if he were about to spit, but instead stuck his gold toothpick in his mouth. "Here, baby," he said to Bathsheba, pulling out a chair for her. "Sit next to these chillun so they can see what royalty feels like." He winked. "You gone just stand there, Charly?"

Charly bent forward and put her palms on the table. She looked around to make sure no one could overhear them. "I'll just stand, if you don't mind," she began, then told Bathsheba and Stax why she'd popped up in Illinois.

She had to be there for her sister, just like Bathsheba and Stax had been there for her many times without even knowing it.

Bathsheba banged her fist on the table as Charly was finishing the story. "If I wasn't a woman of God, I'd kill her. How dare she do that to you chillun? Pretty young ladies like yo'self."

"So she coming with us? Stormy, you coming with us," Smax said.

Charly shook her head. "Nah, I gotta take her back with me, even if I gotta hide her until I can talk my dad into it. But I appreciate it."

Smax shook his head, then gave Bathsheba a look. "Tell her something, Sheba."

"What about school, Charly? How's Stormy supposed to go to school if you hiding her somewhere? School will be here again before you know it. Time goes fast, especially while you're on the road." Bathsheba's eyebrows were high and her arms were crossed.

"Yes, Charly. We didn't think about that? I would have to be enrolled because I can't fail. Failures don't get scholarships. Just like you worked hard for your dream, I want to work hard for mine." Stormy's point was made.

Charly stepped back and looked around. She nodded. Bathsheba was right; she'd wanted to get away so badly and had promised herself she'd never return, and now she was back. She realized she'd returned for more than just to find Stormy, when she took a second to look around. She was surrounded by almost everyone whom she loved and who loved her in return. Bathsheba and Smax had treated her like their own grandchild before she'd moved to New York and become a reality star. Dr. Deveraux El and Rudy-Rudy had been constants in her life, teaching her about stars, universes, and universal law and nations. And Lola, the only best friend she'd ever had besides her younger sister, was the first to give her a reality check. Charly brightened. She'd felt suffocated in the town, as if she had no room to grow and no stage for her dreams; but now she knew she had everything else in Illinois. Friendship. Love. Family. Yes, all the things that counted, she realized as the bell above the restaurant door rang, announcing a customer. Charly looked over her shoulder and smiled. "Make that friendship, love, family, and a *boyfriend*," she mumbled to herself, then excused herself from Stormy and the rest so she could go talk to Mason. They needed to clear the air, and that couldn't happen in the middle of a crowd.

17

Mason wasn't himself, Charly noticed. It'd been less than two months since she'd seen him after the *The Extreme Dream Team*'s first taping in Chicago, but there was something different about him. For one, he seemed taller. Charly raked her eyes over him, wondering what else had changed. She tilted her head, pressed her lips together, and put her hands on her hips. She sniffed. He'd always smelled good, but now his scent was better than usual. More expensive, as if money had an aroma.

"What's wrong with you?" Mason asked, his lips in a half smile. He licked them, then ran his hands over his waves.

Charly nodded. That was it. Mason wasn't wearing a baseball hat like usual. That's what had changed about him. "You just look different. Thinner, taller, something." She rolled her eyes dramatically. "I guess I just missed you. There, I said it."

Mason spread his lips into a full smile. He blushed a little. "Really?" His exhale came out in a half snort. "Even though that Liam dude—"

"Stop it already, Mason," Charly said, cutting him off and pulling him back out of the restaurant's entrance. The breeze blew her hair away from her face as they walked toward the parking lot. "What's your problem? I already told you there's nothing up with me and Liam." She turned toward the back of the restaurant.

Mason grabbed her arm, stopping her. "So that's it? You think you just get to say there's nothing up and I'm supposed to believe you? Even after I saw you and him kiss? Worse, even after the whole world saw you two kiss?"

Charly reared back her head. "Listen. I don't know what else to tell you. I already told you it was scripted. The kiss was scripted," she lied.

Mason laughed, then shook his head in the negative. "Nah, Charly. You've got your dudes mixed up. You didn't tell me that."

Charly exhaled, letting her shoulders sink toward the ground. She was defeated, but she was no quitter. She was going to fight until she won. "So if it wasn't you, it was my dad. Same difference." She threw her hands in the air like *so what*. "Both of you are wrong anyway. The kiss was scripted for Liam and Annison."

Mason looked away, then shot her a glance. Her heart melted because his eyes were tearing. She couldn't believe she'd made him cry.

"I'm sorry," she began, then was silenced by his loud, raw laughter.

"Yo, Charly. I'm no fool," he managed between laughs. "The kiss wasn't scripted. Period." He kicked at loose gravel, then began to walk away.

"Where are you going, Mason? You know I'm not here long. I gotta be back sooner than later, and I still don't know what I'm doing with Stormy. I don't need this now," she said to his back, hoping he'd get over himself.

Mason stopped, then turned around. He licked his bottom lip, then bit it a little, baring his teeth like a dog about to attack. "*You* don't need this now?" He parroted her words, then spat on the ground. "Well, what about me, Charly? You ever consider what I don't need? Let me tell you what I don't need, Charly. I don't need a girl who lies and cheats. There was no script for the award show. You know it and I know it. You and that dude are to-gether—"

"No, we're not, Mason!" she yelled, cutting him off.

Mason laughed again. "Word? Well, what's this then?" He pulled a folded magazine out of his back pocket and tossed it to her.

Charly shrugged. She wasn't a dog, and she wasn't going to fetch anything, especially something thrown at her like a dog biscuit. Her phone rang, and she ignored it.

"What's the matter, Charly? You too afraid to face who you are?" Mason asked.

"Charly! Charly! You okay? TMZ . . . really?" Lola asked, her footsteps getting louder as she made her way to Charly with Stormy on her heels.

Charly looked around. She didn't understand what was going on or why Lola was so out of breath, asking about TMZ. "What?"

"Mason, you know better . . ." The words hung in the air, a statement that came from Stormy's mouth.

"What?" Charly asked again. Her mouth was moving, but her brain wasn't working. Though she wanted to deny everything that was happening in front of her and look into Mason's eyes and dare him to treat her like the scum of the earth again by throwing a gossip magazine at her or calling her a cheater, she couldn't. Her eyes couldn't leave the ground.

"Charly? Answer me," Lola demanded. Her voice was more than concerned. "You okay?"

Charly nodded her head. She and Mason were having a boyfriend and girlfriend disagreement. He wasn't putting his hands on her or calling her out of her name, other than calling her a cheater.

"Yeah," he spat. "Until you can prove otherwise—which you can't—I'm out. One." He turned his back to her, held up the deuces sign, his index and middle fingers displayed in a V, and walked away.

Charly nodded, and a tear tracked down her cheek. On the ground in front of her, in color and black and white, was a huge picture of her and Liam kissing in a car. *It can't be.* "That's impossible," she said.

"So what are you going to do?" Stormy asked, sitting back in her seat inside Smax's.

Charly shrugged. "I don't know. But I'm going to find out who lied on me and Liam. That picture was taken when we—me and the driver—picked him up from Whole Foods in Atlanta. He went to peck me on the cheek and the car pulled off, making him accidentally brush against my lips." She turned the page, then cringed. "This one is when we were leaving the hotel in Miami—we didn't spend the night together! I'm not like that!"

Lola popped her gum, nodding as she pressed the phone against her ear. She moved the cell, then pressed a button. "Sully said he had no idea, but word is spreading. Liam knows, and we're sure Mr. Day does too. You gotta get back."

Charly nodded. "I just don't understand. Why would they print that I'm out to destroy Annison and her career? And over a guy? Liam and Annison aren't even a couple."

Stormy laughed. "You may not think this is funny, and believe me, it's really not. But you wanted to be famous. This is what happens. Reality shows . . . messy shows that mimic messy lives."

Charly nodded her head. Stormy was right. Her life had become a mess, so now it was up to her to clean it up. She'd begin when she made it back. Right now, her sister needed her, and she needed to be home around her family—the crew at Smax's. "Stormy, I was thinking I should stay a couple of days. I'll see if Bathsheba can call the studio for me."

Stormy smiled. "Really? You'll stay?"

Charly nodded. "We're between tapings and don't have another for almost a week." She looked at her calendar. "Most people are flying home, I guess, but some are staying in Florida. Or I can just meet them in Virginia."

18

"They love you, Charly. The audience absolutely loves you—the network too," Mr. Day was saying on the phone, his voice getting more excited with each syllable. "The ratings have been through the roof, and it's thanks to you, Charly. They were higher the first time you filled in for Annison, but they were even higher when Marlow made her appearance. And the tabloids—perfect. I know you don't see it now, but it's just a sign that you've made it. Don't worry about your dad. I'll handle him."

Charly half smiled. She was rightfully upset, but had been pacified. Four networks had contacted her for interviews so she could defend herself, and that'd made her feel better. So had Mr. Day. She'd been avoiding both her dad's and Mr. Day's calls since she'd darted away to Illinois to see about Stormy, and had finally decided to take Mr. Day's call after she'd learned from her voice mail that he was bursting with good news and told her to enjoy her few days at home with her family. Charly smiled. She was thankful for Bathsheba, who had been more than willing to call the studio. Charly was also happy because Bathsheba got information that prevented Charly from flying to the wrong location. It turned out that most of the crew was still in Miami for an all-male show, where Liam and Sully made over an all-boys-school dorm.

"Okay," she said, listening intently as Mr. Day told her how fantastic everyone thought she was, as she sat in a restaurant in Miami International Airport stuffing her mouth with overpriced french fries. One of the cameramen walked by her and waved, then shrugged his shoulders. Charly plastered on a smile, wondering why he shrugged, then held a fry in the air, saluting him with the ketchup-drenched tip in the air. She'd touched down in Miami less than an hour ago and had barely made it to another terminal where she was scheduled to take the next flight out to Virginia with the rest of the cast and crew, but had gotten more strange looks than she could count. She blamed it on the tabloid with the pictures of her and Liam being sold in the airport store. She'd autographed two of them while buying junk food for the airplane ride. "That's great, Mr. Day! I'm happy to hear it. Does this mean Marlow can be on the show? Permanently?"

"The flight's been delayed, love. Or shall I say, lover?" Liam laughed. "Anyway, they're saying something about rain; that's the excuse this time." His voice reached her from behind. His accent seemed to float through the air and tickle her ears, and it sounded absolutely beautiful.

After the rough twenty-four-plus hours she'd spent sneaking in and out of Illinois to check on Stormy, she needed a diversion. She was glad it happened to be him. "You hear me, love?"

She nodded her answer and turned sideways so she could see his face, and a smile spread across hers. She held up a finger to let him know she was on the phone and would be with him in a second. "That's cool, Mr. Day. I'm excited, and I know Marlow will be too. She loves being around people—and not just pet sitters," she said into the cell, happy that Mr. Day had given Marlow the green light to be a part of the reality series. Her eyes saucered when Liam was in her full view, and not because he was his usual gorgeous self. "I gotta go, Mr. Day. I think they're calling us for our flight," she lied, ending the call. "Liam, where's Marlow?" she asked, looking at his hands, which were empty except for the messenger bag he had.

"It's good to see you too, Charly. And you're welcome. You don't have to thank me for watching Marlow or covering for you while you snuck away—or for standing up for your honor and grace and telling the stupid people who keep calling me and my agent that you and I are strictly friends," Liam said.

"Sorry," she said. "I appreciate you. Now, where's my dog?"

Liam shrugged, then pulled out a chair and sat. "I'm afraid there's no more room, love. Seems there were too many dogs booked onboard the cabin. They had to check her with the baggage."

Charly jumped. *Check her?* "Excuse me?"

"Well, it seems there's only a certain number of animals that can be on the plane with the passengers—"

"But we prebooked, right?" Charly asked, sure they had.

Liam crossed his arms over his chest. "The *studio* booked the flights in advance, and according to the reservationist, there was only one kennel ticket booked. Annison got it. I don't know how, but she did. I'm thinking they gave it to her because she's in first class."

Charly crinkled her brows together. He wasn't making sense. "I'm sorry. Did you say she got it because she's in first class? We're all in first class, Liam. You sure it's not because of that stupid gossip magazine? Is that why I'm being mistreated?"

Liam's expression dropped and his head did the twist. He reached over and grabbed Charly's hands. "Listen to me, love. You didn't do anything wrong, and no one is going to punish you." He turned his face, then smiled. "Now, smile for all the people who'll probably report that we're having a lovers' quarrel," he said, nodding his head toward the camera flashes from the cell phones of travelers who'd stopped and were taking pictures of them. "We're not together, and we didn't do anything wrong. After this—this moment—we don't ever have to discuss it again. Okay?" He shrugged.

Charly smiled, then said okay through gritted teeth. She was playing it up for the fans and their cameras just as Liam had suggested.

"Come over here," Liam said to her, patting his lap. "Come sit on my lap and take a picture. I've learned that the best way to make people go away is to give them what they want. The same with reporters—always smile for the paparazzi, take a few pictures and give them short interviews, and they'll leave you alone."

Charly nodded, taking in his advice. "Okay," she said, then got up and rounded the table. She sat on his knee.

"Back to what you were saying," Liam said after the fans left. "Yes, we flew first class to Atlanta and here, to Miami . . . that's true. Just not anymore. I don't know what's happened since, but now only the hosts—the main ones, me and Annison—are flying first class. The rest of the cast, including cohosts, which I think is totally absurd—have to fly coach."

She rolled her eyes. An announcement that their flight was boarding was broadcast over the sound system. Her phone vibrated. A calendar reminder popped up on her screen with a picture of the itinerary embedded.

EVENT REMINDER:
Location Taping
7 AM

THE EXTREME DREAM TEAM
Show 4 itinerary

Recipient information:

Preschool
NAME WITHHELD DUE TO NON-ADVERTISING CLAUSE
Three-year-old preschool that opens its doors to under-privileged.

Enrolls 10 children for free in summer school and free breakfast/lunch programs.

No government grants or public monies given; school does fundraising to support charity.

EXTREME DREAM TEAM Mission: Design and build a new state-of-the-art kitchen, pantry, and 2 classroom additions.

> **Charly's duties:** Assist Annison with design. Mediate between design (Annison) & carpentry (Liam). Communicate with and be responsible for recipients being away from location.

Locale: VIRGINIA BEACH, VIRGINIA

What happened? What was going on? Charly questioned everyone and everything in Virginia. She'd been all but removed from the show, and she couldn't understand why. First, she was given directions to help the local crew that was hired to gather an audience around the set. The producer, some new guy she'd never met, hit her with an excuse that she should interview neighboring businesses to see how they felt about the preschool helping the underprivileged. Then she was asked to take Marlow and Doll for a walk because the pet-sitter/dog-walker had to rush away because of some emergency. Now she was sitting in the truck at a local big-box do-it-yourself hardware store waiting for Eight, Sully's assistant and cameraman, to get his cue to start filming her picking out supplies and bargain shopping. She was disgusted. In less than three tapings she'd gone from cohosting to hosting to who knew what?

Charly pushed open the heavy truck door, then slid out

and down to the ground. Her cute combat-booted feet landed with a thud. She was tired and thirsty and, more than anything else, fed up. "Still nothing, Eight?"

Eight shook his bald head and batted his hairless eyelids. He climbed out of the driver's side of the truck. "Nothing." He walked around to the passenger side and looked at his watch. "We've been here for like four hours. It's almost quitting time," he said. "That's not good. I wonder how Sully's doing."

Charly shook her head. She didn't understand Eight and Sully's friendship, and really didn't see why Sully and Annison got to have an assistant when she and Liam didn't. "Me too," she added. She had a lot going on, but she wanted to know why Sully kept flaking on Lola. Lola was her best friend, so it was only right that Charly look out for her. "How is Sully? I mean, I don't see him much. Is he dating someone?"

Eight shook his head, then laughed a little. "Sully doesn't have time to date. He's busy doing *other* things."

Charly made a face. "Well, excuse me," she said, laughing. "Tell him he could be a little more considerate of my friend."

Eight's phone started ringing. "You mean that weird-looking Lola girl?" he asked, and Charly almost keeled over. She couldn't believe Eight had called Lola weird looking, considering he was the one without body hair. "One sec." He answered his phone, said a couple of okays, I gotchas, and no problems, then hung up. "Well, he likes her. He does. He just can't see anyone seriously right now, Charly. It's not her." He straightened his shirt, then walked away.

Before Charly knew it, Eight had climbed back into the truck and started it. "Where are you going?" she asked through the open passenger door.

"That was a production assistant on the phone. The taping has wrapped."

Charly's eyebrows shot up. "We're doing a two-day taping. That's weird—"

"No. We're done here in Virginia. They've completed the design. Without us. But there is a party later. What's Virginia Beach without the beach?" Eight asked. He'd been laughing while he was speaking, but Charly could tell that he was just as disappointed as she was at not being included in the taping.

19

I'm leaving. Leaving. That's what Charly told herself while she packed her bag and searched for Marlow's collar. "Yes, I'll hold," she said to the front desk, then waited for someone to come on the line who could help her.

"This is the manager, ma'am. How can I help you?" a pleasant voice inquired.

Charly stood tall, as if he could see her. "I'm checking out early, and I need a car to come get me and my dog. The really nice girl who answered, well, she's new and doesn't know if the local cabs around here allow dogs to ride outside of a carrier. Can you find me a car that does, please? I'll be waiting," Charly said, then hung up the hotel phone. Her eyes raked across the room and scanned her cell for a second; she contemplated calling Mr. Day to complain about her suddenly short screen time, but thought better of it. He must have been aware that she wasn't included in the Virginia taping. Mr. Day had known everything since she'd met him, so why would he be clueless about his own show? *The Extreme Dream Team* had been his idea.

Her phone danced on the bed. *Annison* scrolled across the touch screen. Charly waved her hand in dismissal. She couldn't prove it, but something told her that Annison was behind her camera time shrinking and Marlow being flown with the baggage like she was a thing, not a companion. Charly sucked her teeth. She was the last person Charly wanted to talk to, but she had to admit she was curious about what the girl wanted. She shrugged. "Whatever. Right, Marlow?" she asked her faithful friend. The cell vibrated again. This time Liam's name popped up, and she felt compelled to answer.

She leaned over the mattress and picked up the phone. "What's up, Liam? Didn't really get to spend a lot of time with you today. Did you miss me?" Her tone was sweet, but her words were laced with hidden sarcasm.

Liam was mumbling to someone on the other end of the phone, his hand over the cell's microphone, muffling his voice. Obviously he wasn't alone. "One second, love," he said to Charly.

The cell vibrated in her hand, startling her a little. She pulled it away from her ear and looked at it. It was Annison again. She pressed Ignore, then sandwiched it back between her head and shoulder.

"Charly? Love?" Liam called her. "Are you there?"

Charly nodded. "Yes? What's up? Who were you talking to?" she managed to get out in one breath while resuming her packing.

"So you're purposely ignoring Annison's calls then, Charly?" Liam asked, then laughed harder than Charly had ever heard him. He was coughing while he giggled, and she was sure he was holding his stomach, doubled over. Then he started choking, or at least he sounded as if he was. Charly shook her head, then realized that she had joined him. She was just as tickled as he; she just didn't know why, other than because she couldn't help it.

A loud banging on her door pulled her attention away from Liam and his infectious laughter. "One sec," she whispered into the phone, then stiffened.

"Just open the door already, Charly. You can ignore my calls all you want, but I know you're in there," Annison said from the other side of the door.

"Just open the door, love," Liam urged, still tickled. "It's us. Me *and* Annison. Sully will be by after he eats."

Charly rolled her eyes. How dare Liam set her up like that? Something should've told him that she didn't want to be bothered with Annison and that she'd been disregarding Annison's attempts at communication with her for a reason. Ivy League schools didn't roll out the green carpet for nothing, so Liam was too intelligent not to catch on. Better yet, she knew he was smart enough to purposely not tell Annison that Charly had no conversation for her.

Reluctantly, Charly opened her hotel room door. She looked from Annison to Liam without so much as an apology or a guilty feeling in her body. She didn't feel bad for igging her costar—she felt pissed and betrayed.

"Why the 'tude, Charly?" Annison asked, then put Doll on the floor. Her voice was soft, not accusatory like

Charly would've imagined it'd be. If Annison had treated her the way she'd just treated Annison, her words wouldn't have sounded so sugary.

Ignoring Annison's question, Charly looked at Doll, then smiled. Doll and Marlow would prove to be just the diversion she needed as she watched them romp around on the floor.

"Wow! You must be really angry," Liam said, walking past her, then going over to the bed and plopping down. He picked up a shirt. "What are you doing, packing or finding something to wear tonight?" he asked, roaming his eyes over the mess she'd made on the bed. "Oh. A suitcase. Guess that means you're packing then."

Charly's hotel phone rang. She looked over at it, then ignored it. She didn't know why she was so popular all of a sudden, but she could do without it. Her day had been horrible, and her week hadn't been too fabulous either. She did want to be famous, just not all the time.

Annison walked over to her and purposely bumped her shoulder into Charly's. "Well, at least I'm not the only one you're ignoring," she said, biting back a smile. "But if I were you, I'd answer it. It's important. Call me psychic," she advised.

Charly cut her eyes at Annison, then threw Liam a death stare. They were up to something, and she didn't like it, whatever it was. The two of them had never been close before, so she didn't see the reason for them being so friendly now. She walked over to the makeshift desk that was attached to the wall. "Yes," she answered, picking up the hotel phone.

"Charly? I know you're upset, and you have every

right to be. I don't know what happened today, but I can promise you that it won't happen again." It was Mr. Day. His breathing was heavy, like he was out of breath, and the tone of his voice said he was more than angry. He was irate. "I talked to the . . . never mind. Let me deal with the executive office; the business end is for adults. Now, can you do me a favor? Please tell Annison and Liam that you're okay. They decided they're going to boycott the next taping if you're not involved the way you should be. Especially Annison, who made it a point to call the exec offices, and without her . . . well, you know," he said, then hung up the phone before she could say a word.

Annison walked in front of her as Charly put the phone back on the hook. She crossed her arms, then sneered a little. "Well? Say it . . ."

Charly reared back her head, knowing what *it* was, and hating herself for assuming her being excluded from the rest of the Virginia show was Annison's fault. She calmed herself, then made her shoulders relax. She shook her head. "Okay. I'm sorry, Annison. I don't know why, but I thought it was you."

Annison shrugged, then sat on the bed. She stretched out her body next to Liam's and propped her head on her hand. "Why? Why does everyone always think I'm such a bad person?"

Liam laughed. "Really, Annison? You don't know?"

Annison shook her head. "No, it's just kind of always been that way. Ever since I was little, people always assumed I was the bad guy. I think because I was popular and on television—people always mistake me for having that only-child syndrome."

Charly scratched her head, then looked at Liam. He shrugged. "Aren't you the only child?" he asked Annison.

"Aren't you?" Charly parroted.

Annison laughed, covering her mouth. "No. I have two brothers and a sister, and they're all younger, so, if you ask me, they're the spoiled ones. They were handed everything—including careers. I'm the one who made us famous; they made it because of my name and fight to the top. So, really, I'm the only one who has to work for a living." She threw Liam a look. "Out of curiosity, Liam, a few seconds ago you looked like you know why people assume I'm the bad guy. Share."

Charly looked at him, waiting. She didn't know why Annison was always assumed to be the bad guy, and now felt guilty for having chalked her up to being a devil who did evil without reason. She'd begun to equate Annison with meanness, like *tiger* with *stripes*. Some things just went together. She knew it was unfair, but hadn't been able to help it with Annison. Certain people just triggered certain things—like Mason now triggered her guilt and school principals triggered respect. She wanted to kick herself to check herself. She, of all people, should've known better. Back in Illinois, she'd been mistreated because people thought that she thought she was better than others, when that hadn't been the case at all. She'd just had a case of the Ambitions, and it made others feel *less than* because Charly was always pushing forward. "Yes, Liam? Please do. I'm curious because it's happened to me too. I've been a victim and also guilty of hanging the innocent." She flashed Annison an apologetic smile, which Annison returned.

"Okay, here's why," Liam offered, nodding. "But after this, we have to get ready for the party. The reason everyone convicts you of crimes, Annison, is the same reason they've convicted you"—he pointed to Charly—"and will convict you even more now, Charly. So both of you pay attention to this. You're both stars, and beautiful ones at that. People love to hate celebrities and they hate to love them too. Think about it." He eyed Charly. "Look what the tabloids did to us. And we can't blame pretty little Annison here. We know for a fact that she was in bed, half dying from food poisoning."

Charly's hotel phone rang again, and she remembered she'd called the front desk. Quickly, she answered. "Sorry . . . I won't be needing a car after all. But do you know of any great local dog sitters who'll pet sit in my room?"

20

Charly sat near a cove, sticking her feet in the tide that rushed to the shore with nighttime intensity. Her ankle-length skirt was pushed up to her thighs, covering her swimming suit–clad body. Just about everyone else seemed comfortable, but she was too cold to walk around half nude. She didn't care if she was on a beach or not; she wasn't going to freeze for anyone, not even the local entertainment reporters who were there to interview the crew. From where she sat, she could see everyone having a good time, and wished she could join them. Sure, she could physically be there with them, doing the exact same things they were doing, but mentally she couldn't participate. Something was still off, and not knowing why she'd been cut from the Virginia taping and why Marlow had been restricted to riding with airplane luggage baffled her. Mr. Day had said that the ratings had skyrocketed because of her and that the network executives had fallen for her, so why would she be practically cut out of the show?

"You okay, love?" His voice startled her. "What, you're missing your dog too much? Don't worry. She's got an excellent dog sitter," Liam assured her.

She'd been so busy concentrating and trying to figure out what went wrong, she hadn't heard Liam approach. She nodded her head. "I'm good. I'm just trying to breathe for a minute. I'm not really feeling the party."

"You or Annison. Did you hear all that commotion she was making? Seems she left her phone at the hotel, and is trying to send someone to get it. Guess her flunkies aren't going for it tonight." Liam stepped out of his shoes, then rolled up the bottoms of his jeans. "You mind?" He sat next to her and extended his feet until they were stretched past hers, then tried to touch his ankles, stretching. "I'm too tight from working out," he explained, unable to complete the stretch. He leaned back on one elbow, and drew in the sand with his free hand. Charly could tell he was thinking or planning something, she just couldn't tell what. "I have something to tell you," he said, then stopped dragging his index finger across the damp beach. "Do you mind?" He looked at her with intense eyes that danced in the moonlight.

Charly nodded, watching him closely. She never could put her finger on what it was about Liam that attracted her, but it was much more than his accent and his looks. He'd thrown her off earlier by bringing Annison to her room unexpectedly, but she still trusted him for some reason. "I'm listening." She sat up, then turned and faced him.

"You like me," he said, smiling arrogantly and know-ingly.

Charly reared back her head and laughed nervously. "Wow. That was a little too you-think-you-know-me. And about my boyfriend . . . ? Aren't you concerned that I have one?" she began, getting ready to tell him what had happened with her and Mason.

Liam shook his head in the negative. "I didn't bring him up, and no, I don't know that you have one," he said sarcastically. "Do you, love? I don't see him anywhere around and I don't hear you talk about him. So how much of a boyfriend can he be?" He looked at her, then placed his hands on the ground and pushed himself up to his feet. Standing, he reached out to her. "C'mon, let's walk."

Charly took his hand and stood. No, she didn't know. She didn't know a lot of things anymore, like who lied on her and Liam to the gossip magazine and was following them from city to city to take pictures; or what was going to happen to Stormy if her father didn't allow her little sister to move in with them when Charly returned to New York. She wasn't even sure about what happened with the show, though she knew Mr. Day was going to take care of it and she was going to have more camera time. Charly began to walk next to him, then noticed he was walking like he was in pain.

Suddenly he stopped, grinding his feet into the damp sand. A boathouse was close by and the party was far off, barely in sight, but muffled sounds could be heard. "I hate to do this, and I know you Americans frown upon it, but I have to warn you about something. And no, I'm not doing this because I want your boyfriend's position—even though I do—but I'm telling you this because you're my friend," Liam said, looking her dead in the eyes.

Charly gulped. She hadn't told Liam that she and Mason had broken up. In fact, she'd tried to forget that day in the parking lot at Smax's because it hurt too much. She and Mason had been best friends once, and he'd treated her like a stranger. He knew she wasn't a fast girl; she was just ambitious about her career. Still, she couldn't believe Liam was going to drag Mason through the mud to make himself look better. She thought it was a cheap shot and had expected more from Liam. She put her hand on her hip and pursed her lips. "What? I guess you're going to tell me Mason's doing something wrong? Just like the tabloids said *we* were, huh?"

Liam smiled, then leaned forward. He shrugged. "I was going to tell you this." He kissed her for real. It wasn't like the fake kiss someone had photographed from somewhere outside of the car at Whole Foods in Atlanta. It was a real-life, I-really-like-you kiss. "I was only going to warn you about me. I like you . . . I mean, I really like you, Charly. And I'm going to do everything I can to win you from him. He may be a cool dude, but I'm better for you. Trust me."

Charly smiled. "Well, Liam . . ." she began.

"Hey, you two! There you are. Come on. Nobody has time to wait for y'all." Sully's deep voice cut through the air. Charly couldn't see his face, but there was no getting around his rudeness, and she could make out his silhouette. It seemed that morning yoga had him chiseled. "Mr. Day's been looking for you," he barked.

Charly turned and looked in Sully's direction. "We're coming!" she yelled back, then grabbed Liam's hand, pulling him along as she ran toward the party. "Hurry." She looked over her shoulder, then her eyes moved toward the boathouse. Her eyes saucered and a chill climbed her. She stopped midstride and pointed. "Liam, do you see something over there?"

Liam laughed. "No, nothing but water and shadows and, of course, speedboats. I'm afraid that's that Illinois or New York coming out of you, love. You guys are so paranoid." He stumbled.

Charly nodded. "Paranoid, or we just listen to ourselves . . ." She looked at Liam in the darkness. "Why are you in so much pain?"

Liam waved her away. "I told you back there. I've been working out too much without stretching. You saw I couldn't touch my toes."

Charly laughed. "Well, you can call me paranoid, but I can call you stubborn. You need to do like Sully," she said, stopping and putting her hands on her hips.

Liam reared back his head, and his voice changed. He was more serious than Charly had known him to be. "What do you mean, be like Sully?" The look he wore was one of disbelief. "If anything, Sully wants to be like me. He likes you."

Charly laughed. "Nah . . . he likes my best friend, Lola. They've been talking a lot. A whole lot."

Liam nodded. "Ah, that's good. That means I can be his friend again," he joked. "Okay, maybe not. He's not a big fan of mine." He shrugged. "Then again, Sully's not a fan of anyone. So, now, what about me needs to be like Sully?"

Charly grabbed his hand. "Yoga. If you did morning yoga, you wouldn't be in so much pain."

Liam laughed. "Yoga's for girls. I thought I told you that before. Sully doesn't do yoga . . . he can't. Not while we're on the road—at least not with the girls."

Charly threw him a nasty look. "That's sexist—"

"No, love. That's the rules around here. The girls do yoga—that's per Annison's dad—"

"What do you mean, per Annison's dad?" Charly asked. She knew Mr. Day listened to the parents, but even she thought Annison's dad having control over everybody was a bit much. Charly's dad called the shots concerning his daughter, not the crew, and her dad was not to be played with. "I get he's a big shot at the network, but why does her dad get to say what goes on with the cast?"

Liam laughed. He folded over and grabbed his middle, cracking up. "Not just a big shot. Since he bought his way into the studio last year, he's part owner and now the biggest honcho at the network. He doesn't just input, he now calls all the shots. All of them!" he said, straightening up. They began to walk again. "And trust me—no guys do yoga. Period. Her dad is so strict that he hired a private yoga instructor for his little girl, who travels with us. Daddy dearest doesn't want any boys to see his daughter in tights. There's nothing he won't do for her. Nothing. Including getting her that poor little dog that she neglects so much so she could look like a Goodwill Ambassador of rescued dogs." He shook his head. "You know how much of a pet lover she is? She loves that dog so much that she's caged her up in that room and hasn't fed her in two days. I overheard that earlier."

"What? Days? Locked in her kennel without food and water? She'll die," Charly said, upset and even more disgusted.

"Yes. But what can I do? If I report her . . ."

Charly nodded. She got him. If he reported it, his career was as good as flushed down the toilet. Annison was dirtier than she'd imagined, but she could play dirtier. She wasn't afraid of Annison or her dad. It all was starting to make sense now. Her dad may not have the money Annison's dad did, and he may not have been in her life since she was born. But now that they were reunited, she knew without a doubt that there was nothing her father wouldn't do for her either, especially to protect her.

Charly stopped walking. She had to save Doll, and knew just how to do it. She grabbed her middle and moaned just a little. "I don't feel good, Liam. Do you mind if I skip the party?"

Liam eyed her. "You sure? You need me to call a doctor?"

Charly shook her head. "No, thank you. But can you apologize to everyone for me? I'm not going to be able to make it to the party. I'll see you at the hotel . . . in the morning. I need to get as much rest as I can tonight, so I'll be ready for the show tomorrow."

She whipped out her phone, then sent a text:

Answer your phone and pretend to be Annison. The hotel will be calling to verify.

21

EVENT REMINDER:
Location Taping
Tomorrow 11 AM

<u>THE EXTREME DREAM TEAM</u>
Show 5 itinerary

Recipient information:

Humanitarian and Community Service builders
The RED & WHITE HOUSE c/o Howard University
College-aged females
Sorority sisters
Helps the local community and contributes to national community service, raises money for local scholarship fund.

EXTREME DREAM TEAM Mission: Design and build an updated study area and an enclosed porch on the sorority house.

> **Charly's duties:** Assist Annison with design. Mediate between design (Annison) & carpentry (Liam). Communicate with and be responsible for recipient being away from location.

Locale: WASHINGTON, D.C.

Charly looked at her phone and nodded. She'd almost forgotten about the taping tomorrow. She'd been so upset, and had been piecing it all together, that everything else had slipped her mind. All she could think about was saving Doll and that she'd been betrayed, and questioned why. Nothing else mattered—except making sure Doll was taken care of and her sister was okay, but even Stormy would have to wait until she talked with her father. Right now, she needed to concentrate. Think and plan. The car pulled up to valet parking at the hotel, and a nice gentleman opened her door. "Thank you," she said to the driver and hotel man, then got out of the car. Marlow was upstairs with the sitter, so she knew she had time to do what she needed to do. The sitter wasn't expecting her back for hours, she thought, looking at her watch as she made her way through the lobby and beelined straight to the desk.

"Excuse me," Charly said to the front-desk attendant. "My name is Charly St. James, and I'm with *The Extreme Dream Team*. I called and spoke with the manager earlier. He gave me the name of a local pet sitter, who's in my room now watching my dog," she said, pulling identification out of her purse, sliding it over the counter. "I'm not here for myself. I need to get into Annison Reynolds's room. It seems her dog is alone, and I need to get her out before she makes a mess of the place." She made a yucky face. "She's not trained yet. Also, you can call Annison to verify," Charly said, giving them Lola's number. She wasn't worried about them having Annison's on file. The star's cell phone number wasn't usually given out.

The card key didn't work. Charly stomped her foot, unable to believe it. She was irritated and nervous. She looked at her hand, then realized she'd slipped it into the lock backward. She tried again, and a green light popped on by the door. "Yes!" she said in a loud whisper, then pushed open the door. Doll's whimper met her ears before she set foot in the room, and she shook her head. "Doll," she sang, sniffing the air. The room smelled of perfume and dog poop, and Charly's stomach turned. Not because Doll had used the bathroom, but because she knew Annison had her locked away in some tiny, cute carrier that would look good on her arm or in photos. "Poor Doll," Charly said, following the dog's cries to the bathroom and seeing she was right. The dog's kennel was tucked in the corner of the bathroom, stuck under the counter that housed the sink. "Sorry, baby," she said, bending down and sliding out the carrier that had some designer's initials all over it in capital letters. In seconds she'd removed the tiny dyed-red dog and set her in the tub. She turned on the faucet and released a lukewarm light flow of water so Doll could drink and not freeze from it being too cold. She looked around for some sort of shampoo, specifically puppy shampoo, but didn't see any. Sure that the dog couldn't get out because she was too small, Charly ran into the bedroom to see if she could spot any toiletries there. A brown and beige oversized duffel that matched Doll's carrier pulled her attention, and she walked to the corner. As she went to reach for it, a piece of paper—with Charly's name written in all capital letters across the top with a red Sharpie—caught her attention.

PLEASE SEND TO CHARLY FOR THE D.C. SHOW

REVISED (Charly)

THE EXTREME DREAM TEAM
Show 5 itinerary

Recipient information:

Humanitarian and Community Service builders
The RED & WHITE HOUSE c/o Howard University
College-aged females
Sorority sisters
Helps the local community and contributes to national community service, raises money for local scholarship fund.
EXTREME DREAM TEAM Mission: Design and build an updated study area and an enclosed porch on the sorority house.

Charly's duties: ~~Assist carpentry (Liam and Sully).~~
~~Communicate with neighborhood crowd.~~ *NONE!!!!!*

Locale: WASHINGTON, D.C.
*PS: The spy store recorder worked. Found out her sis-
ter's alone at home. Inform child services that her sister's
been abandoned. If her sister needs her, she'll have to
leave the show. I won't be upstaged by someone like her!*

Suddenly the door burst open and Annison barged in.

"What are you doing breaking into my room?" Annison yelled, then stopped.

Charly just looked at her, then held up the note. Mr.
Day and Liam rushed in behind Annison.

"Charly, is that really you?" Mr. Day asked, even
though he knew it was she. "Annison, I owe you an apology. Charly, you have a lot of explaining to do—"

"Something's wrong! Charly wouldn't just break in
here. I know her better than that," Liam stressed, looking
at Charly. "Right, Charly?"

Charly shook her head, then smiled knowingly. "Mr.
Day, it seems you've been tricked. Annison wasn't going
to walk if I wasn't on the next show. She's the reason I
wasn't on the last one." She held up the note, then stood.

Her walk was menacing as she handed the note to
Liam and Mr. Day, then darted toward Annison. "So you
were going to get my sister taken, Annison! Do you not
know who I am? I'm from the South Side," she declared.

EPILOGUE

Annison's head was bandaged and her face was scratched. She sat on the edge of the hospital bed, swinging her feet. She shook her head, then hung it.

Charly sat across from her in the cold, hard chair. She couldn't stand the girl, but felt more sorry for her than anything. In her hand, she held pictures of Doll and Marlow. "So, are you better?" she asked.

Annison nodded her head, then shook it. She was clearly confused. "I'm getting better, but my head still hurts. I really thought you were going to kill me."

Charly laughed. She'd gone after Annison, who'd run like the wind. Charly knew the girl was strong from years of constant yoga practice, but she hadn't known she was so fast. Annison had hightailed it out of the hotel room before Charly could get to her, then down the hall. Liam had tried to hold Charly back, asking her to stop and saying he didn't want her to go to jail. While he was holding her, Annison had run down the stairs, through the lobby, and then had collided with the glass doors, thinking they were open. "I wanted to, but it doesn't make sense. You've been doing a good enough job on your own. Karma, ya know. It comes back."

Annison nodded, then shrugged. She was no longer the self-assured, egotistical star everyone held so high. Her being caught had somehow stripped her of all her pride, and now she sat before Charly looking helpless. Tears tracked down her cheeks. "I'm sorry, Charly. I didn't mean to hurt you . . . and I really didn't want to hurt your sister, either."

Charly cleared her throat. "And Doll? Mason?"

Annison shook her head. "Doll? Well, I really wanted Doll. She was so cute that I just had to have her, and I really planned on taking care of her, but I couldn't. I've never even taken care of myself. There was always someone to do it for me."

Charly shrugged. She wished she could say the same, but she couldn't. She now had her father, though. He and Stormy, and that was all she needed. She still didn't have Stormy's issue resolved, but she'd get to it later. "And . . . ?" she asked, inquiring about Mason.

Annison shook her head. "How did you know?"

Charly laughed. "Yoga. One, you never invited me *and* him. You invited just me, and you didn't say when or where we were going. Then all of sudden, there he is, which meant you and he must've been talking. And two, I found out no guys were allowed to go to yoga, which meant there was something up . . . you had to sneak him

in, and knew when to do it because your regular instructor wasn't there."

Annison nodded. "I don't know if you're able to, but
I'd like you to keep Doll. She's sweet, and I'll be willing
to help pay her way."

Charly held up her hand. "Mason?"

"You're good, Charly. Really good," Annison said.
"But if it helps any, I didn't really want Mason. He was
just someone to talk to . . . another way to get—"

"To get me off the show, I know. But why? What did I
do to you?"

Annison scooted to the edge of the bed, then slid off.
For a second Charly thought they were going to come to
blows, because it seemed as if Annison was standing her
ground, no matter how shaky and dirty it was. Her eyes
narrowed, her breath deepened, and her chest rose and
fell. The tears continued to flow while her nostrils flared.

Charly lunged toward her, then grabbed her tightly.
She pulled Annison to her, embracing her in a hug. Annison broke down and began sobbing like a baby. "It's
okay," Charly said.

"I didn't want to, Charly," Annison said. "There was
just so much pressure. I couldn't let my dad down. He's
the head of the network, so I can't be a failure," Annison
began, then told Charly she'd never really wanted to act,
and as soon as she found a way around it, Mr. Day and
her dad had come up with the show; then Charly upstaged her.

Charly let Annison go and smiled. "Well, you should've
said that in the first place," she said. "What do you really
want?"

Annison smiled. Believe it or not, I just want to be regular. I want to go to college, spring break . . . all the things other kids my age do."

Charly nodded. "So you'll go to college. I can promise you that. With your conniving ways and my strength, you're good to go. I gotcha!"

Stay tuned for Charly's next epic fiasco!

REALITY CHECK

Kelli London

ABOUT THIS GUIDE

The following questions are intended to
enhance your group's reading of
REALITY CHECK.

Discussion Questions

1. Sometimes a girl has to do what she has to do! Charly had to fight for what she wanted—she risked getting in trouble with her dad, who was against her acting until school was out; she snuck into the studio to fake-it-to-hopefully-make-it and revealed the real Annison. Do you see anything wrong with how Charly handled getting what she wanted? Do you think there were other ways she could've gone about it? How would you have handled it?

2. Discuss a time when you wanted something as badly as Charly. What did you do and what was the outcome?

3. Charly believed that life is what you make it, and she never backed down or let anything deter her, not even Stormy's situation. How do you handle life's disappointments and obstacles?

4. Boys can be trouble, but they can also be good. Mason seemed like a bad guy and Liam seemed good. Do you think that Mason was really bad and out to hurt Charly? Or was he a victim of the circumstances that came with Charly's stardom? Do you think that Liam was really the good guy or too good to be true?

5. In *Reality Check* we saw that family, whether biological or chosen, is very important. Charly had
   Lola, Smax, Bathsheba, Dr. Deveraux El and the
   rest of Smax's crew, and her life wouldn't have
   been what it was without them. How important is
   family to you? Where would you be without them?

6. Charly's dad seemed very rigid and didn't appear
   to be a supporter of her dreams. Do you think
   that was really the case or was he just concerned
   about her education and well-being?

7. When a teen doesn't listen to their parents, they
   can be labeled a problem child. Do you think
   Charly was a problem child because she didn't listen to her father in the beginning of the book and
   went after her dream without his permission? Is
   there another way she could've handled it, even
   after she knew she couldn't talk him into it?

8. Almost every teenage girl has some sort of problem with a parent. And Charly's mother didn't fit
   the definition of mother at all. However, a mother
   and daughter relationship is sometimes very important to a girl's life and self-view. Do you think
   there's a way for Charly to mend her relationship
   with her mother? Should she?

9. Charly wanted stardom. Stormy wanted education. What do you want?

Please read on for an excerpt from

Vol. 1 of

Charly's Epic Fiascos.

In stores now!

1

This is going to be easy. Simple. "Turn. Turn. Turn!" Charly said, grabbing her little sister, Stormy, by the forearm. She shoved her hip into Stormy's side, forcing her thin frame to round the corner of the schoolyard. Her feet quickened with each step. They were almost home-free.

"Ouch!" Stormy hissed, cradling her torn backpack to her bosom like an infant in an attempt to prevent her books from falling onto the cracked sidewalk. "All this for Mason? Serious? Let go of my arm, Charly. Let me go. If I had known we'd be up here mixed up in drama, I wouldn't have come to meet you. I need to get home and study."

Charly rolled her eyes. Being at home is exactly where her sister needed to be. She hadn't asked Stormy to meet her. In fact, she remembered telling her not to come. She'd had beef with one of the cliques over nothing—not him, as Stormy thought. Nothing, meaning the girls were hating on Charly for being her fabulous self and for being Mason's girl. She held two spots they all seemed to want but couldn't have. She was the It Girl who'd snagged the hottest boy that had ever graced her town. "Go home, Stormy," she said, semi-pushing her sister ahead.

"Do it again and I'm going to—" Stormy began.

"You're going to go home. That's all you're going to do," Charly said matter-of-factly, then began looking around. She was searching for Lola, her best friend. If she had to act a fool, she'd prefer to show out with Lola around, not Stormy. She had to protect her younger sister, not Lola. Lola was a force to be reckoned with and she wasn't afraid of anyone or anything.

A crowd came her and Stormy's way, swarming around them as the students made their way down the block. A shoulder bumped into Charly, pushing her harder than it should have. Charly squared her feet, not allowing herself to fall. Quickly, she scanned the group, but was unable to tell who the culprit was. "If you're bad enough to bump into me while you're in a group, be bad enough to do it solo. Step up," Charly dared whoever.

Stormy pulled her as some members of the crowd turned toward them. "Come on, Charly. Not today," Stormy begged. "Remember the school said if you have one more incident you'd get suspended."

Charly grabbed Stormy's arm again, preparing to jump in front of her in case the person who pushed her stepped forward.

"Hey, baby," Mason called, pushing through the crowd. "Everything good?" he asked, making his way to her and

Stormy. "Or do we gotta be about it?" he asked, then threw a nasty look over his shoulder to the group. " 'Cause I know they don't want that." His statement was a threat, and everyone knew it. Just as Charly was protective over her sister, Mason was protective over her. His lips met her cheek before she could answer him.

"We're fine, Mason," Stormy offered.

Mason nodded. "Better be. They're just mad 'cause they're not you. But you know that. Right?"

Charly smiled. Yes, she knew.

"Good. Listen, I need to run back into the school for a minute," he said, reaching down for her book bag.

Charly hiked it up on her shoulder. "You can go ahead. We're good. I promise."

He stood and watched the crowd disperse and start to thin before he spoke. "All right. I'll catch up to you two in a few." He disappeared into the crowd of students still on school grounds.

"So really, Charly? You were going to fight whoever over him?" Stormy asked again.

Charly ignored the question as she focused on parting the crowd. They needed to get down the block.

"Hey, Charly! Call me later. There's something I want to talk to you about," a girl shouted from across the street.

Charly looked over and nodded. She couldn't have remembered the girl's name if she'd wanted to, let alone her number. Obviously the girl knew her though, but who didn't?

"Catch up with me tomorrow," she answered, then released her grip on Stormy and sucked her teeth at her sister's questioning. Stormy had no idea. Mason was the new guy around and the guy of her dreams. They'd been dating, but she couldn't let him know just how much he had her because then she'd be like every other girl in their town. And she refused to be like the others, acting crazy over a guy.

"Mason, Charly? That's what this is all about?" Stormy asked again.

"Shh," Charly said, shushing her sister. "What did I tell you about that? Stop saying his name, Stormy."

Stormy shook her head and her eyes rolled back in her head. "Serious? What, calling his name is like calling Bloody Mary or something? I *so* thought that Bloody Mary thing only worked with Bloody Mary's name and Brigette's generation. Who believes in such stuff, Charly? You can call anyone's name as many times as you like."

Charly got tense with the mention of their mother. Brigette refused to be called anything besides her given name, and Mom, Mommy, and Mother were definitely out of the question. That she'd made clear. On top of that, she insisted her name be pronounced the correct *French* way, Bri-jeet, not Bridge-jit.

"Please don't bring her up. My afternoon is already hectic enough. I don't wanna have to deal with Brigette until I have to," Charly said, her quick steps forcing rocks to spit from the backs of her shoes. "Just c'mon. And, like you, I need to get my homework done before I go to work. Mr. Miller said if my math assignment is late one more time, he'll fail me. And I can't have that. Not right before we go on break for a week. And I don't want to do any sort of schoolwork while we're out. Oh!" She froze.

A dog ran toward them at top speed from between two bushes, then was snatched back by the chain leash around its neck. It yelped, then wagged its tail, barking. Charly, a little nervous, managed strength and pushed Stormy out of harm's way. Looking into the dog's eyes, she was almost afraid to move. She'd distrusted dogs since she was five, when her mother had convinced her they were all vicious, and now her feelings for them bordered on love/hate. She'd loved them once, and now hated that they made her uncomfortable, but was now determined to get over her fear. A pet salon near her home was hiring, and, whether she liked dogs or not, she needed more money for her new phone and other things.

The wind blew back Charly's hair, exposing the forehead that she disliked so much. Unlike Stormy, she hadn't inherited her mother's, which meant on a breezy day like today, her forehead looked like a miniature sun, a globe as her mother had called it when she was upset. On her mom's really peeved days, which were often, she'd refer to Charly as Headquarters. Charly smoothed her hairdo in place, not knowing what else to do.

Stormy grabbed her arm. "C'mon, Charly. We go through this at least twice a week. You know Keebler's not going to bite you, just like you know he can't break that chain." She shrugged. "I don't know why you're so scared. You used to have a dog, remember? Marlow . . . I think that's the name on the picture. It's in Brigette's photo album."

Charly picked up speed. Her red bootlaces blew in the wind, clashing against the chocolate of her combats. Yes, she'd had a dog named Marlow for a day, then had come home and found Marlow was gone. Charly had never forgotten about her, but, still, she'd believed her mother then, and now couldn't shake the uneasiness when one approached. Especially Keebler. He'd tried to attack her when he was younger, and she still feared him. So what if he'd gotten old? Teeth were still teeth, and dogs' fangs were sharp. "How do you know he won't bite, Stormy? You say that about every dog."

Stormy laughed, jogging behind her. "Well, Charly. Keebler's older than dirt, he doesn't have teeth, and that chain is made for big dogs, I'm thinking over a hundred pounds. Keebler's twenty, soaking wet. What, you think he's going to gnaw you to death?"

Charly had to laugh. She'd forgotten Keebler was minus teeth. "Okay. Maybe you're right. We only have two more blocks," she said, slowing her walk. Her pulse began to settle when she caught sight of the green street sign in the distance, and knew she'd soon be closer to home than barking Keebler. "Only two more and you can get to your precious studying, nerd," she teased Stormy, who laughed. They both knew how proud Charly was of Stormy's intelligence. Stormy didn't hit the books because she needed to; she had to, it was her addiction. "And I can knock out this assignment," she added.

"Yo, Chi-town Charly! Hold up!" Mason called, his footsteps growing louder with each pound on the concrete.

Charly picked up her pace. She wanted to stop but she

couldn't. Boyfriend or not, he had to chase her. That's what kept guys interested. Stormy halted in her tracks, kicked out her leg, and refused to let Charly pass. "What's going on now? Why are you ignoring Mason? Oops, I said his name again." Stormy sighed, pushing up her glasses on her nose.

Charly rolled her eyes. "I'm not really ignoring Mason, Stormy. Watch and learn—I'm just keeping him interested," she said, failing to tell her sister that she was trying to come up with an explanation for disappearing the weekend before. She'd told him she was going to visit her family in New York, and now she just needed to come up with the details. Her chest rose, then fell, letting out her breath in a heavy gasp. What she'd hoped to be a cleansing exhale sputtered out in frustration. "He may be a New Yorker, but we're from the South Side of Chicago. I got to keep the upper hand." She repeated the mantra she used whenever she had to face a problem, but it was no use. The truth was, yes, they had been born on the South Side of Chicago, but now they lived almost seventy miles away from their birthplace in an old people's town. She couldn't wait to leave.

Mason's hand was on her shoulder before Charly knew it. She froze. Turning around was not just an option; she had to. She knew that he knew that she'd heard him now. Summoning her inner actress, she became the character she played for him. Charly switched gears from teenage girl to potential and future Oscar nominee. She erased the glee of him chasing her down from her face and became who and what he knew her to be. Cool, calm, self-assured Charly—the girl who seemed to have it all. Seemed being the operative word since she lacked teen essentials like the Android phone she was saving for and a computer.

"Hey! I said hold up. Guess you didn't hear me. Right?" His voice was rugged and his words seemed final, as if he had nothing else to say. His tone spoke for him. It was sharp and clipped, yet something about it was smooth. Just hearing him speak made her feel good.

She smiled when she turned and faced him. "Hi, Mason. I'm sorry. There's so much wind blowing that I couldn't hear you."

Mason smiled back and did that thing with his eyebrows that made her melt every time. He didn't really raise or wiggle them, but they moved slightly and caused his eyes to light. "Yeah. So . . ." he began, then quieted, throwing Stormy a *please?* look.

"Okay. Okay. Personal space. I get it," Stormy said, then began to walk ahead of them. "You high schoolers are sickening."

Mason smiled at Stormy's back, and Charly grimaced behind it. She hadn't asked Stormy to give her and Mason alone time, and wished that her sister hadn't. The last thing she wanted was to be alone with Mason because every time she was, her lies piled. They'd stacked so high that now she couldn't see past them, and had no idea how to get around or through them.

"So, I've been trying to catch up with you to see how New York was last weekend when you went to visit your pops. You did fly out for the weekend, right?" he asked, his eyes piercing hers like he knew she hadn't gone.

She scrunched her brows together. It was time to flesh out her partial untruths. She thought of her semi-truths that way because to her they were. She'd done and been and imagined it all in her head, so, in a way, her not-so-trues were kind-of-trues.

"Uh, yeah." *Here comes the hook*, she thought while she felt the fattening lie forming on the back of her tongue, pushing its way out her mouth. "Right. But it was no biggie. I wasn't even there a whole two days. I was in and out of Newark before I knew it. I visited my dad and my aunt. She works for a television station— where they film reality shows. One day I'm going to be on one. That's the plan—to become a star."

"Newark? That's Jersey. I thought you said you were flying into Queens." He looked at her, pressing his lips together. He'd totally ignored her star statement.

"Queens? Did I say Queens?" *Dang it*. She shrugged, trying to think of a cover.

"Yep. You said your pops was picking you up at La-Guardia airport. That's in Queens. Guess Newark was cheaper, huh?" He waved his hand at her. "Same difference. Me and my fam do it too. Sometimes it pays to fly into Jersey instead. It's about the same distance when you consider traffic time instead of miles."

Charly nodded, pleased that Mason's travel knowledge had saved her. "Yeah. I know that's right. And I got there when traffic was mad hectic too. I'm talking back to back, bumper to bumper. But it was cool though. Manhattan's always cool, Brooklyn too," she lied about both. She'd never been to Manhattan and she was only five when she'd visited Brooklyn. But she'd gone to places like Central Park and Times Square all the time in her mind, and a mental trip to the Big Apple had to count for something.

"Brooklyn, yeah, it's cool. Matter fact, I miss home so much, I just got a puppy and named her Brooklyn." He smiled.

Charly raised her brows. "Really? That's hot. I just love dogs. In fact, I just applied for a gig working at the pet salon." Another partial lie. She had planned on applying, she just hadn't had time yet.

Nodding in appreciation, his smile grew. "That's good, Charly. And it couldn't have come at a better time." He took her book bag from her, then slung it over his shoulder. "Dang. This is heavy. What'chu got in it?"

"Math," Charly said. "I got to ace this assignment, so I brought home my book and every book the library would let me check out to make sure I get it right. Because I go to New York so much, I kind of fell behind on the formulas," she added. She couldn't have him think her anything less than a genius.

Mason nodded. "Good thinking. Knock it out from all angles. Math is the universal language. Did you know that?" he asked, but didn't give her time to answer. "Let's walk," he said, clearly not letting up. "It must be nice to have your pops send for you a couple times a month. So what'd you do all weekend? Party?"

She kicked pebbles out of her way, wishing they were her lies. She hadn't seen her father since she was five, and it was something that was hard for her to admit, especially since Stormy's dad was still on the scene for birthdays and holidays. The truth was she had no idea where her father was, so she imagined him still living in New York, where she'd last seen him.

"So did you party?" Mason repeated.

Me, party? Yeah, right! My mom partied while I worked a double to save for a new phone. Then I sat holed up in the house on some fake punishment. "Yeah, actually I did. Nothing big though. It was a get-together for my aunt. You know, the one I told you about who's a big shot at the network. Well, she just got promoted, and now she's an even bigger big shot. She's got New York on lock."

Mason nodded, then slowed his pace as Charly's house came into view. "That's cool, Charly. Real cool. It's nice to finally have a friend I can chop it up with. Ya know, another city person who can relate. Somebody who gets where I'm from. Not too many people around here can keep up with my Brooklyn pace," he said, referring to the almost-dead town they lived in. Their tiny city was okay for older people, but teens had it bad. They lived in a nine-mile-square radius with only about twenty-five thousand other people. There was only one public high school and one emergency room, which equated to too small and everybody knowing everyone else and their business. Nothing was sacred in Belvidere, Illinois.

Charly took her book bag from Mason. "Trust me, I know. They can't keep up with my Chi-Town pace either. I'm getting out of here ASAP."

He walked her to her door. "Speaking of ASAP. You

still gonna be able to come through with helping me with my English paper this week? I have to hand it in right after break, so I'd really like to get it finished as soon as possible. Don't wanna be off from school for a week and have to work." He shrugged. "But I know you're pressed with school and getting an A on the math assignment. Plus, with flying back and forth to New York to check your pops, and trying to work at the pet salon, I know you're busy. But I really need you, Charly," he paused, throwing her a sexy grin that made her insides melt. "I don't even know what a thesis statement is, let alone where one goes in an essay."

Charly smiled, then purposefully bit her tongue to prevent herself from lying again. She'd forgotten when Mason's paper was due. An essay she would be no better at writing than he would. She sucked in English, but couldn't pass up the opportunity to be close to him. "I gotta work tonight and pretty much all week," she said. She was finally kinda sorta truthful. She did have to work. Now that she was sixteen, and had snatched up a job at a local greasy spoon—and, hopefully, the pet salon she'd told him she had applied at—it was up to her to make sure that the electric and cable bills were paid, plus she had to pay for her own clothing. "We've been *very* busy at work, for some reason."

"Okay." Mason grimaced, then looked past her, apparently deep in thought. He rubbed his chin. "I don't know what I'm going to do now. I gotta pass this class. . . ."

Charly pressed her lips together. She couldn't let him down. It was because of her that he'd waited so long to tackle the paper. She'd told him not to worry, that she had him, that she was something like an A or B English student. Now, it'd seem as if her word was no good, and she couldn't have that.

"Kill the worry, Mason. I'll work it out."

2

"Charly!"

Before the front door closed behind her, Brigette's voice ambushed her from somewhere inside the house. Probably upstairs in the bedroom, Charly assumed. Ninety-nine-point-seven percent of the time that's where her mother took up residence. Brigette's wide hips were either spread out on the bed or else swishing down the staircase toward the kitchen, where she kept up with her never-ending caloric intake. "Charly! *Char-lee!* Is that you? Don't you hear me talking to you, girl? Stormy was in here thirty minutes ago. Where've you been? Hunh? If you had time to waste, you better have used some of it to pay cable. *Did* you pay the cable bill? All the stations aren't coming in—it's nothing but static on the flat screen. And I gotta record my vampire flick and soaps, you know that."

Charly exhaled, closed the door, and dropped her

heavy book bag on the floor. She hiked her shoulders, flexing her muscles until they tightened, then released them. She was trying to force her blades to relax, which wasn't such a good idea. It was really an oxymoron, as Stormy had pointed out many times, because you couldn't force and relax at the same time.

"Smile. Smile. Smile," she told herself, trying to make herself feel happier so that Brigette wouldn't accuse her of having a disrespectful tone. She couldn't speak to Brigette if she allowed her true emotions to surface. "Ma'am?" she called out, lightening her voice so it wouldn't reflect the you're-already-getting-on-my-nerves attitude she had.

Five raps sounded at the front door, followed by a short pause, then three more knocks. *Lola.* Charly's best friend was making her usual appearance, announcing herself with the sound of eight, the amount of letters in her full name. Lola Dowl, no middle name or initial.

"Ma'am? Don't ma'am me when I'm calling you, Charly. Get your grown butt up here and help me slip into this girdle!" Brigette yelled.

Charly eased the front door open with a hand on her hip and a sinister smile.

Lola raised her brows, pursed her lips, then walked in. Her shock of naturally bleached-looking blond curly hair was all over her head as usual, and her cinnamon skin, which Charly had never seen blemished, glowed more than normal, making her light blue eyes glow. "Hmm. You don't even have to tell me. Your look says it all. Let me guess. Brigette's in one of her I'm-laid-off-and-pissed-at-the-world moods again?" Lola asked, setting her designer leather messenger bag on top of Charly's antique thrift-store book bag. Lola was superstitious and would never set a purse, or anything resembling one, on the floor. She believed if she did so, she'd go broke.

"Charly! I. Said. Is. That. You?" Brigette yelled again.

Stormy's pretty face popped around the corner, where she faithfully studied in the dining area. She smiled at Lola and shook her head at Charly. "Awful. Just awful. I'll be so glad when she goes back to work. You better hurry, Charly. Hurry up so you can work on your math," she reminded, pushing up her glasses on the bridge of her nose, then disappearing.

Charly waved Lola on. "Come on. You can wait in my room until I see what she wants. Probably some soda," Charly said, calling pop soda like the New Yorkers she'd heard on television.

"Yes, you better hurry, Charly. I heard Mr. Miller's been on one lately. They said his wife left him for another man, and ever since then he's been flunking everybody." Lola pushed back her blond porcupine-looking hairdo, reached a hand into her pocket, then pulled it out, balled up in a fist. She extended it toward Charly. "Here."

Charly reached out her hand to take whatever it was Lola was giving. "What's this?"

Lola released a wad of bills onto Charly's palm. "Uncle Steely's staying with us for a while."

Charly nodded, clearly confused by Lola's statement. "Your uncle's staying with you. Oh . . . kay? I'm not following."

"Hurry up, Charly! And bring that greedy Lola with

you," Brigette hollered. "I know she's here. She always is, like she don't got a home. Heck, I should claim Lola on my taxes as much as she's here and eating up all the food I work so hard to buy!"

Charly gave Lola an apologetic look as they walked through the living room, passing the old-school thirty-two-inch television, and made their way to the steps. "Sorry. Now what were you saying about your uncle?"

Lola waved away Charly's apology. "Sorry for what? Don't be. I'm not. *You* buy all the food I eat!" Lola covered her mouth and laughed. "I don't take Brigette serious." Lola's smile faded. "Uncle Steely. Don't you remember him? He's the one that steals any and everything not bolted down, including people's identity." She shrugged. "So I can't keep your money for you anymore 'cause when he steals it—and he will steal it, trust me—I can't afford to replace three hundred dollars."

Charly nodded at Lola's reasoning, and wished she were old enough to go open a savings account on her own, without Brigette's signature. "Two hundred and eighty-six bucks," she said, counting the last of the dead presidents, then shoving the wad into her pants pocket. "I won't have the rest of the cash for the phone—or the hundred-dollar cable bill Brigette keeps ragging me about—until Friday because I had to pay the electric company. But, thanks for keeping it as long as you did, Lola. If Brigette knew . . ."

"Oh, I know. It'd be spent at the mall or deposited in her account," Lola finished Charly's statement. "That's only two days away. I sure hope it hurries up and comes, for your sake. You can't keep walking around talking on that old clunk of a phone. Not with everyone thinking you're the ish!" Lola laughed.

"Charly . . . I'ma count to ten, and if you're not up here . . ." Brigette threatened.

Charly just shook her head and quickened her pace. She didn't feel like dealing with Brigette today or any day, truth be told. Her mom was a trip, and because she'd had Charly when she was sixteen, Brigette seemed to forget that she was the parent. Instead of a daughter, Charly was more like Brigette's maid and personal handmaiden, or like a roommate who footed bills but had no say, *and* a live-in nanny for Stormy, which Charly didn't mind. As far as Charly was concerned, she and Stormy were better off without the lady who'd given birth to them. It was peaceful and loving when she wasn't around, and when she was home it was hell.

Brigette was a modern-day demon-licious witch, complete with cascading fake hair and too ample cleavage, courtesy of the G-cup over-the-shoulder-boulder-holder she wore and, Charly finally realized that, like her, her mother was also a liar. So maybe, just maybe, Charly had inherited the dishonest gene because there were many things wrong with Brigette's barrage of questions and statements. One, Stormy had walked in the door only a couple of minutes ahead of Charly. Two, if there was "only static" showing on the television, how were "some" of the stations coming in? Three, no one could "slip" into that contraption her mom had called a girdle. It wasn't really a girdle, it was some magic bodysuit sort of thingy that two or more people had to literally tuck Brigette's fat inside, then she'd have to sleep in it for a day or two to *look* ten pounds lighter and a couple of sizes smaller. Four, Brigette hadn't actually called Charly to her; she'd only said her name and asked if *that* was Charly. And five, Lola was right; Brigette didn't buy most of the food they ate. In fact, Brigette was laid off, so how could she be working so hard to buy food?

Charly raised one foot high, then rushed it toward the floor with all her might, stopping short of stomping it on the carpeted stair. She then lifted the other, repeating the pretend stomp over and over with alternate feet, making her way up to her mother's bedroom and wishing that she could bang hard enough to make the stairwell shake. But as much as she wanted to pound her soles on the floor, she couldn't. Brigette, besides being a semi-lazy half-caring mother, was also a bit mentally unstable. She'd earned a reputation in her teenage days that still followed her. Brigette wasn't to be messed with. She'd been known to drag a woman or two down the street, face against the pavement, had cut more than one of her boyfriends, and had even made a policeman cry. Charly inhaled. No, she wouldn't test her mother. She may not have been her biggest cheerleader, but she was no fool.

"Ma'am?" Charly repeated again, cracking open the door to her mother's bedroom and sticking only her face inside the room. Lola pushed her all the way inside, causing her to almost trip and collide with her mom's backside. "You called me?" Charly's question came out in a sputter as she caught her balance, barely missing running into her mother's huge rear end.

Brigette was bent over, her panty-covered butt and

dented thighs facing Charly and Lola. Her head was up-side down between her legs, and her face was barely visible beyond her nose because her boobs were in the way. With perfectly drawn-on brows, she scratched the scalp of her lace-front wig with inch-long acrylic nails, making the expensive hair move side to side as if she'd grown it.

"Why you so nervous all the time, Charly?" she asked, her face peeking between the inverted V her thick legs were opened in. Unsuccessfully stretching her hands toward her feet, she seemed stuck, and had apparently been trying to lace up high heels that tied in a crisscross around her calves. The size of her gut prevented her from bending all the way to accomplish the task. There was just too much stomach to allow her full access to the laces. She let out a *whew*, unfolding herself to a stand. She stuck out a foot. "Tie this up for me. I don't know what's going on. For some reason, I'm a little winded today."

"Yeah, right. Too much weight," Lola muttered, lowering her tone with each word, and making Charly giggle.

Brigette snaked her neck. "What the . . . ? What did you just say, you lil' fast heffa?" she barked at Lola.

Lola smiled and shrugged her shoulders. "Nothing, Ms. Brigette. I only said it's not *right*. If you put on the shoes now, it'll be harder to put on the girdle. And . . . I wouldn't want anything to happen to those shoes. They're really nice."

"Yeah. Those are nice, Brigette," Charly enthusiastically agreed, not meaning a word of it. The shoes were atrocious, and looked like a pair of high-heeled Egyptian sandals that someone had once worn in Anytime B.C.

Brigette straightened until she looked taller, then squared her shoulders. She lowered her lids to a squint, and looked at Charly as if she was trying to figure out if she was being truthful or not. Her nose wiggled; then she scrunched it, raising her top lip toward her nostrils like something was stinking. Sucking her teeth, she put her hands on her hips, then stuck out her foot farther, twisting it side to side. She smiled. "Yeah. But they're more than nice. I paid almost two hundred for these." She snapped her fingers, then pointed to the magic bodysuit on the bed. "Get that bottom piece, Charly, and let's get this over with. I got a hot date, and I need to be breathing by the time he gets here. It's a new one with a panty and upper. It just came in the mail, so you know what that means. It's new so it'll take a couple hours just to inhale right."

Charly did as she was told, then squatted, stretching out one leg opening of the contraption as much as she could while her mother stepped in. Lola followed suit, grabbing the other side of the girdle. She nodded at Charly, indicating she was ready. With all of their strength, they stretched, tugged, pulled, and hiked the too-small girdle out and over and up Brigette's thick thighs and hips, then proceeded to work on part two. Wrapping the what'cha-ma-jig over her stomach and breasts, they tucked in the excess fat where they could and patted what they couldn't until it was flat as possible to help disguise the weight.

"And the fat is gone, baby. Gone! Yeah. Whew," Brigette sighed like she'd done some actual work to fit into the contraption that only disguised and reassigned her fat to different sections of her body, and not made it disappear like she believed. Holding her head high, she whirled to her full-length mirror, switching her walk to that of a runway model. She tossed her hair, did a full spin, then turned back sideways. She gave herself another once-over. "See this?" she asked, patting her now-flatter tummy. "Gone!" She moved her hands over her huge breasts, then trailed them down her middle, moving them to her back, and rounded them over her butt. "A work of art. Curves like these will make a blind man dizzy. I'm so chiseled even a man who can't see *can* see this Coca-Cola bottle shape!"

Charly crinkled her brows and looked at an equally confused-looking Lola. "All right. Can I go now, Brigette?"

Brigette froze. "Uhm. Let me see. . . ." She looked at Charly, deep thought registering across her forehead in wrinkles. She put her finger to her temple, contemplating. "Hell no! This house needs to be cleaned. My sheets need to be changed, and the toilet . . . when was the last time you gave my toilet a good hand wash?"

Lola shook her head. *Run, Charly! Run!* she mouthed, not uttering a sound.

Charly's phone did a jig in her pocket, then began chirping. With each sound it got louder and louder. "My job alarm," she explained to everyone, turning toward the door so she could run and change into her work uniform. "Brigette, I gotta get to work." Her words were apologetic. "Okay?"

Brigette laughed. "Okay? Okay? Heck, someone around here has to punch a clock, and since I'm laid off, who better than you? You can clean up when you get home tonight. And you better learn how to hustle faster than you have been. How you gonna work at the plant with me making cars, if you don't? You know you ain't smart enough for college, so you might as well come with me. That is, if they call us back to work."

Lola grabbed Charly's arm on their way out of Brigette's bedroom. "Don't worry about your math, Charly. I had Mr. Miller last semester, and I know what it takes to get a high grade. I'll do your homework for you."

Charly wrapped Lola in a sisterly embrace. "I owe you one!" she said, then began hopping out of her pants on the way to her room. She threw them in the corner, then reached for a pair of tights. Her stomach growled. "And as long as I owe you . . ."

"Yeah. I know. I know. As long as you owe me I'll never go broke. I've heard that before, but I still only got lint in my pockets," Lola said, picking up Charly's shoes and handing them to her. "I'll meet you at your job later. I know my moms isn't cooking. And you know I gotta eat."

HAVEN'T HAD ENOUGH? CHECK OUT THESE GREAT SERIES FROM DAFINA BOOKS!

DRAMA HIGH

by L. Divine

Follow the adventures of a young sistah who's learning that life in the hood is nothing compared to life in high school.

THE FIGHT ISBN: 0-7582-1633-5	SECOND CHANCE ISBN: 0-7582-1635-1	JAYD'S LEGACY ISBN: 0-7582-1637-8
FRENEMIES ISBN: 0-7582-2532-6	LADY J ISBN: 0-7582-2534-2	COURTIN' JAYD ISBN: 0-7582-2536-9
HUSTLIN' ISBN: 0-7582-3105-9	KEEP IT MOVIN' ISBN: 0-7582-3107-5	HOLIDAZE ISBN: 0-7582-3109-1
CULTURE CLASH ISBN: 0-7582-3111-3	COLD AS ICE ISBN: 0-7582-3113-X	PUSHIN' ISBN: 0-7582-3115-6

THE MELTDOWN
ISBN: 0-7582-3117-2

SO, SO HOOD
ISBN: 0-7582-3119-9

BOY SHOPPING

by Nia Stephens

An exciting "you pick the ending" series that lets the reader pick Mr. Right.

BOY SHOPPING ISBN: 0-7582-1929-6	LIKE THIS AND LIKE THAT ISBN: 0-7582-1931-8	GET MORE ISBN: 0-7582-1933-4

DEL RIO BAY

by Paula Chase

A wickedly funny series that explores friendship, betrayal, and how far some people will go for popularity.

SO NOT THE DRAMA ISBN: 0-7582-1859-1	DON'T GET IT TWISTED ISBN: 0-7582-1861-3	THAT'S WHAT'S UP! ISBN: 0-7582-2582-2

WHO YOU WIT'?
ISBN: 0-7582-2584-9

FLIPPING THE SCRIPT
ISBN: 0-7582-2586-5

PERRY SKKY JR.

by Stephanie Perry Moore

Inspirational series that follows the adventures of a high school football star as he balances faith and the temptations of teen life.

ICE X	PRESSING HARD ISBN: 0-7582-1872-9	PROBLEM SOLVED ISBN: 0-7582-1874-5
FRAYED UP 0-7582-2538-5	PROMISE KEPT ISBN: 0-7582-2540-7	